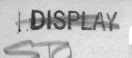
DISPLAY
STO

ALLEN COUNTY PUBLIC LIBRARY

S0-EBU-988

"Your job is to plan my wedding!"

Max insisted angrily, not wanting Emma exposed to any danger. His mention of the wedding stopped them both for a moment.

Emma stared him down. "As I said earlier, Max, you don't have any say in what I do. And I am not going to stand by as everyone accuses you of being a thief."

"I am a thief."

She whirled on him passionately, her face ablaze with anger. "Not anymore. You've changed. You said so yourself. You're an honorable man. Even leaving me at the altar was, in your opinion, a noble action."

"An honorable man. Is that what I am? Then you don't know me at all." Max was furious. Angry at Emma for her pigheadedness. Angry at himself for feeling emotions for her that he didn't feel for Meg.

He grabbed Emma and pulled her body close to his. "Would an honorable man, one who's getting married in less than two weeks, do this?"

He crushed his lips against hers....

Molly Liholm has an unusual hobby called "briding." Once a year, she and a group of friends gather on a beautiful June day with picnic baskets in hand and travel to a local park to catch the brides and their flocks of bridesmaids. As Molly and her friends bride-watched and invented and then told imagined stories about the happy couples (and the in-laws and ushers and other wedding-party members), Molly was inspired to write the tale of Emma Delaney and how she handled her disasterous wedding. Thus THE GETAWAY GROOM was born.

A Toronto native, Molly worked in publishing for years before starting to write romance fiction. She swears that the publishing characters in this book have absolutely no resemblance to anyone she has ever met in her sixteen-year publishing career!

Books by Molly Liholm

HARLEQUIN TEMPTATION
552—TEMPTING JAKE
643—BOARDROOM BABY

Don't miss any of our special offers. Write to us at the following address for information on our newest releases.

Harlequin Reader Service
U.S.: 3010 Walden Ave., P.O. Box 1325, Buffalo, NY 14269
Canadian: P.O. Box 609, Fort Erie, Ont. L2A 5X3

THE GETAWAY GROOM
Molly Liholm

Harlequin Books

TORONTO • NEW YORK • LONDON
AMSTERDAM • PARIS • SYDNEY • HAMBURG
STOCKHOLM • ATHENS • TOKYO • MILAN
MADRID • WARSAW • BUDAPEST • AUCKLAND

If you purchased this book without a cover you should be aware
that this book is stolen property. It was reported as "unsold and
destroyed" to the publisher, and neither the author nor the
publisher has received any payment for this "stripped book."

For Erik Vallik
with lots of thanks for all his help,
especially when it comes to computers.
Congratulations on deciding to become a groom!

ISBN 0-373-25772-4

THE GETAWAY GROOM

Copyright © 1998 by Malle Vallik.

All rights reserved. Except for use in any review, the reproduction or
utilization of this work in whole or in part in any form by any electronic,
mechanical or other means, now known or hereafter invented, including
xerography, photocopying and recording, or in any information storage
or retrieval system, is forbidden without the written permission of the
publisher, Harlequin Enterprises Limited, 225 Duncan Mill Road,
Don Mills, Ontario, Canada M3B 3K9.

All characters in this book have no existence outside the imagination of
the author and have no relation whatsoever to anyone bearing the same
name or names. They are not even distantly inspired by any individual
known or unknown to the author, and all incidents are pure invention.

This edition published by arrangement with Harlequin Books S.A.

® and TM are trademarks of the publisher. Trademarks indicated with
® are registered in the United States Patent and Trademark Office, the
Canadian Trade Marks Office and in other countries.

Printed in U.S.A.

Always a bridesmaid…

"PACK YOUR WEDDING DRESS, I need help planning a wedding!" the familiar voice announced over the phone. Bridal consultant Emma Delaney tried to put a face to the voice, but it wouldn't materialize. She received similar requests several times a month, but this wasn't just a regular client playing with the name of Emma's incredibly successful business, Have Wedding Dress, Will Travel. She and her two employees arranged weddings, although that was really an understatement. What Emma guaranteed was that she would take the headaches and worries off the bride's shoulders, ensuring the star of the event basked in the glow of her special day.

Emma knew from firsthand experience what it was like to have your wedding day turn into the worst day of your life.

Suddenly an image of the face that went with the voice began to form in Emma's mind. Thick brown hair, brown eyes hidden behind glasses, a pale face with no makeup. "Meg Cooper? Is that really you?"

"It's me." Meg's laugh held warm, honeyed tones. At college, that laugh had made men take more than a second look at Meg. "Don't tell me you'd given up on me ever walking down the aisle, just like my family had?"

"I never predict marriages anymore," Emma said firmly. There had been a time when she had—and look at that disastrous result. But she did wince a little at Meg's question.

They were both thirty-two, an age that did seem to put a woman well past the blushing-bride stage. Moreover, Emma was surprised that Megan Cooper was concentrating on a man long enough to marry him! Throughout Meg's life, at school and at work, her friend had lived in her world of books. She had always preferred fictional heroes to any of the real men she dated. Emma sighed. Who could blame her?

Emma leaned back in her comfortable, green leather chair—it added just the right executive touch to a business that could seem too feminine—and continued her conversation with her old friend. Had it really been almost three years since she'd last seen her? "Now I only plan the most fantastic weddings."

"Can you put one together in two weeks?" Meg asked, sounding nervous.

Emma had once organized a society wedding in twenty-four hours, but even so, two weeks was short. She liked to include extra time in every wedding schedule for the inevitable unexpected problems, but too frequently brides called her as the approaching nuptials loomed, panicking because too much was still left undone. Emma was known, after all, as the professional wedding saver. "Two weeks. It can be done. But is there some reason for the rush?" she asked, probing delicately.

"Oh, not that," Meg said quickly, obviously understanding that Emma wondered if she was facing a maternity deadline. "Frasier and I are planning an *old-fashioned* wedding night."

Emma was surprised, because she knew that beneath Meg's scattered exterior lurked a very passionate woman. Why, one semester she'd decided she needed to improve her...*romantic technique* and her boyfriend had walked around with a silly grin on his face—when he wasn't asleep in class. "Frasier must be a very special guy."

"Oh he is, Emma. I know you two are going to love each

other. But it's just that, well..." Megan stopped and Emma could imagine her playing with a pencil, tapping it against a desk, in the same nervous manner she'd had at school. Emma and she had both been English lit majors and had shared many classes, as well as being dorm mates in their freshman year. Sharing many of the same interests and ideas, they'd quickly become friends. But there were also fundamental differences between them. While Meg frequently lost herself in her books and her research, seeming the cliché of the absentminded bookworm, she was also very practical, even conservative in her goals and objectives. Emma, who from outward appearances seemed practical, was the dreamer, the real romantic. And look where it had gotten her. Planning other people's weddings!

Meg took a deep breath, then hurried on. "I sort of forgot to do anything about the wedding. I was so worried about the launch of D.C. Hatfield's new book—and the whole fall list had problems—and then I found this great new writer who needed a lot of work and..."

If it had been anyone else but Megan Elizabeth Cooper, Emma would have known that this was a case of wedding denial—of a bride or groom completely unsure whether she or he was doing the right thing—and she would have packed her bags and arrived to help find a graceful way out of the wedding. That was the unique aspect of her business. She wanted happy endings for her clients and that sometimes meant canceling a doomed marriage.

But Megan could very easily have forgotten about her own wedding if she was worried about her job as editorial director of Scorpion Books. Emma remembered how Meg had missed more than one essay deadline and exam because she'd been so involved in another project.

"When Frasier and I decided to get married three months ago, the date seemed so far away," Meg explained.

"Have you done *any* of the preparations?"

"My secretary seems to have sent out invitations, but he's a man and doesn't know much else about organizing a wedding. Oh, Emma, all these people have RSVP'd and I don't even have a dress! Frasier is used to my...peculiarities, but I can't tell him I forgot my own wedding date! Please, Emma, you have to help me. I don't know what else to do."

"I'll be on the first train out of Philadelphia in the morning." A train meant she could bring a lot of supplies with her—fabric swatches, her files on New York caterers, photos of centerpieces and floral arrangements. "Where are you holding the reception?"

"I don't know," Meg said miserably. "All we told the guests on the invitation was the date and the time, like celebrities do with their secret weddings. I thought I could work out all the details later."

"Well, this certainly is *later*," Emma said with a note of amusement, aiming to calm her client and friend. "Don't worry, I can arrange a lot in two weeks." That, after all, was the reasoning behind the name Have Wedding Dress, Will Travel. An inveterate fan of television shows new and old, she had stolen from the classic TV Western *Have Gun, Will Travel*. Just as the cowboy hero had advertised his willingness to travel anywhere to help those in need, so Emma promised to help any bride in need. She certainly knew just how awful a wedding day could become if you didn't have help.

"Oh, thank you," Meg said, and burst into tears.

Emma let her cry for a few minutes while she tried to work out the train schedules. "I'm going to bring a lot of stuff with me, so can you meet me at your father's house in Long Island at 11:30 tomorrow?"

"Yes." Meg sniffed and blew her nose. "Maybe we could have the wedding at Daddy's place."

Daddy's place was a mansion. Peter Cooper was a self-made millionaire. "See?" Emma said. "Things are coming together already. Are you still a size eight?"

"Yes."

"Brown hair, brown eyes, glasses?"

"Highlighted hair. Contacts. Horn-rimmed glasses only when I want to appear intellectual." Meg giggled, probably in relief, because she'd never been much of a giggler. Serious and determined was how Emma had always thought of her.

"You'd be surprised at how well a pair of glasses can fool a person," Meg added.

Emma wouldn't be surprised at all. She knew only too well that people saw what they wanted to see. What their first impression told them. She'd never been able to learn much more about Maxwell Thorne, the man who had betrayed and humiliated her. Pulling her thoughts out of her annoying and foolish past, she said, "I'll bring some dresses. I think I have something you may like." Cradling the cellular phone against her shoulder and continuing their talk of preferred styles of wedding gowns, Emma left her small office for the showroom. She rented a large space in central Philadelphia so that she could offer full service to brides—including their choice of wedding and bridesmaid dresses, floral displays, invitations. Photos lined the walls, documenting the wide range of nuptials she had arranged, including formal society weddings, garden weddings, a theme wedding à la Anthony and Cleopatra and an adventure wedding on top of a mountain.

Clients were impressed by the quantity and variety of merchandise in her store, but her secret was that her inventory cost her next to nothing. She was always on the search for young designers. In exchange for exhibiting their work, she got dresses, shoes, veils and hats on a consignment basis. She sent so much business to typographers, engravers and gift shops that they happily provided her with sample books of their work.

As Emma crossed the showroom, she saw Beth in the sitting area—emerald green couches and a washed-pine coffee table—drinking tea and conferring with a client. Her other full-time employee, Susan, was at a wedding at the Plaza. It was the first wedding Susan had organized by herself and so far everything seemed to be going well—no panicked call-waiting beep interrupted Emma's conversation with Meg.

Emma strode over to the rack of gowns, thinking she had one that might be perfect for Meg. "You're still tall, aren't you?"

Meg laughed. "The only thing about me that could make me a model is my height. Oh, thank you, Emma."

"Wait until you see what I've got. An ivory gown with a fitted bodice and lots of décolletage. You'll look beautiful. And don't worry, we can put on a fantastic wedding in two weeks."

"All I want is for it to not be an embarrassment. Dad's got enough problems with the company to worry about."

Now Meg sounded very concerned, and Emma wasn't surprised. Megan Elizabeth Cooper had always known that one day she would work at her father's publishing company. In fact, Emma had always assumed that Meg would inherit the leadership of Scorpion Books. Meg passionately loved her family's business. So much so that Emma was pleased man had been able to inspire her to even greater passion. Frasier had to be a very special man. "Meg?" she murmured in concern, wanting her friend to feel free to unburden herself about the corporate problems, but not wanting to pry too much.

Meg sighed. "It's why we've all been so distracted, even Frasier. It'll be good to talk to you, Emma. I think I could use your advice."

"If you're getting cold feet about the marriage, honey..." Emma began, wondering if she'd read Meg wrong.

"Agreeing to marry Frasier is the smartest thing I've ever

3. 1833 03151 7698

done," she announced, sounding much brighter, more confident. "It's the company—"

"Scorpion Books."

"Yes, there's something wrong." Emma could imagine Meg taking the ever-present pencil from behind her ear and turning it over and over again. "I don't know the specifics, but Daddy is acting really weird. At first I thought it was because my father has finally met a really nice woman, but...something not right is happening at Scorpion. You know how much the company means to Daddy. To me." She stopped, and Emma could imagine her strong friend pulling herself together. Then Meg began again much more brightly. "I'll tell you about it tomorrow. And you can meet Frasier. I know you're going to love him. Everyone does!"

As EMMA MANEUVERED the rental van to a stop at the front door, she saw that the Cooper mansion was as wonderful as she'd remembered. Meg had invited her to visit once during a school break. Being a small-town girl, Emma had never seen a mansion before, much less slept in one. Since then, having planned several important society weddings every year, Emma had visited far grander houses, but she had warm memories of Meg's home. She was glad that the Cooper house still looked magnificent.

The Grecian style mansion with its Corinthian columns stood on a five-acre estate. Five acres of beautifully manicured lawn with trees planted at strategic points to provide shade and shelter from prying eyes on the road. Emma took a deep breath, cherishing the smell of flowers and fresh-cut grass. She sneezed and remembered one of the reasons why she liked living in the big city of Philadelphia. She'd deliberately left small-town life behind, but having a country home was a pleasant fantasy. She wondered if Phillip Jones was still the head gardener. She'd need his help with the flowers.

The massive oak doors opened and Meg flew down the steps. She hugged Emma tightly, and suddenly Emma was desperately glad to see her friend again. When Emma had arrived at college, fresh from her teeny, tiny town in Kansas, school had frightened her. While she had a naturally gregarious personality, at first the sheer size of Philadelphia, the speed and the energy, how worldly the other students seemed, had overwhelmed her. Meg was the first good friend Emma had made. Quietly she had shown Emma how to fit in.

Although they'd been good friends, their very different careers and the fact that Meg lived in New York while Emma stayed in Philadelphia meant that they'd seen little of each other since graduating. The last time they'd been together was at Emma's grandmother's funeral three years ago. She vowed to change the careless pattern they'd fallen into. Meg might soon become a married woman, but Philadelphia wasn't all that far from New York.

"I'm so glad you're here." Meg had the polished shine of a successful woman. In burnt orange suede pants and a chocolate brown cashmere sweater, she was bending the country-dressing rules just enough to please herself. She had always dressed for herself, but now the results had a lot more pizzazz.

"Wow," Emma exclaimed, surveying her shiny auburn hair, her bright eyes. "Being engaged sure does agree with you. You look fabulous."

"Maybe it's my last few days of independence that are putting that extra bounce in my step." Meg laughed, and Emma expected the entire male population of Long Island to suddenly materialize out of the trees, lured by the husky sound of that voice.

"I still can't believe you took your nose out of a book long enough to find a husband." Emma unlocked the back door of the green van. The color, her favorite, perfectly matched her green chenille sweater and long flowered skirt. She loved fall dressing. Silly as she knew it was, she'd taken the color of the van to be a good omen. Sort of her own version of, *Yes, this wedding can be saved*. The inside of the vehicle was filled with files, boxes and garment bags. "I brought some dresses to show you—you'll have to make a decision on those right away. Beth will arrive tomorrow with the rest."

Meg blinked. "There's more? Oh, my. I never knew there were so many things..."

Emma took her friend's arm and steered her toward the house. "First, I need a coffee. Then you can tell me all about Frasier. And then we'll get someone to help us unload those boxes." They passed the marble entranceway and took a hall that Emma remembered led to the kitchen. "There!" She pointed at a solid mahogany door she knew led to the library, which also served as Mr. Cooper's study. "Maybe we can turn that into wedding headquarters."

Meg chuckled. "Daddy will die. I'll ask Phillip to move the boxes there. Serves Daddy right for insisting on a big wedding. Let me find Phillip while you go to the kitchen."

The kitchen was wonderful. Large windows took up most of one wall, and a long, rectangular table sat next to it. Emma loved the sheer size of this kitchen and all of its conveniences. Two king-size refrigerators held her in thrall for a minute. Imagine! Two fridges. She opened one but was disappointed to find it held only condiments, no wheels of cheese or baskets of fresh strawberries. Well, she supposed Mr. Cooper was really the only one who lived here full-time. He'd never remarried after the death of his wife, when Meg was only a teenager. Meg had an apartment in Manhattan, a few blocks away from the office. Jay, Meg's younger brother, was never in any one place long enough to call it home, although Emma supposed he'd find his way back for Meg's wedding.

Still, Emma wished the Coopers could see their house as

she did. To them it was merely home, but to her it was her every fantasy, having been an only child raised by her grandmother. Abby Delaney had loved her and had done her best with Emma—and Emma had been crushed when she passed away—but Emma had frequently fantasized that her parents hadn't really died in a car crash when she was only two. Instead she'd pretended they were simply away—working for the government had been one of her favorite stories. She'd imagined her parents as glamorous spies, living in a mansion like this one, throwing fabulous parties, exchanging witty repartee. And then one day they would return for her and she would join them at the big house.

Emma found the coffee-espresso maker but could only stare at its myriad buttons in bewilderment until Meg walked in. "Let me," she said. "I only figured out how to work this contraption after we did a book on coffee."

"You were always like that." Emma sat down gratefully on one of the wicker kitchen chairs and watched Meg's economical moves as she measured out milk and finely ground, dark coffee beans.

"Like what?" Meg asked as she began to steam the milk.

"Figuring out how to do things from a book."

Meg poured out equal amounts of coffee into two large cups and then ladled the frothy milk on top. She sprinkled a little bit of cocoa on the mixture and carried the two cups over to the table. Emma tasted the coffee; it was perfect, of course. "I'm a little surprised you didn't buy a copy of *Martha Stewart's Wedding Planner* and put on the whole show by yourself."

"You're ignoring my bad habit of losing myself in my projects and forgetting the real world exists." Meg sighed and fingered her silver earring. "But you're right, I could have thrown something together. Only Daddy has gone off half-cocked and invited everyone he knows, even the aunts from Atlanta."

Emma almost choked on her coffee. "The aunts from Atlanta?" Peter Cooper's dislike of his dead wife's sisters was well-known to anyone who knew the family. Apparently the duo had opposed the match and had tried to convince Lily not to marry the no-good carpetbagger. Lily and Peter had eventually eloped and enjoyed fifteen years of wedded bliss. As Peter Cooper grew more successful, as he managed to buy Scorpion Books and turn it from a small, money-losing specialty press into a successful commercial publishing house, the two sides of the family had reconciled. Except for the aunts from Atlanta.

"And they're coming?"

"Apparently they wouldn't miss it." Meg paused, tapping her coffee spoon against the marble countertop. "It's just that I have this feeling, Emma. Like when I want to publish a book by a writer no one's ever heard of and I just know, in my gut, that it's going to be a hit."

"But you don't have a good feeling about the wedding?" Emma surmised. Meg nodded. "Has your gut ever been wrong?" Meg shook her head. "So, what you're really hiring is my disaster-proof guarantee?" she asked gently.

Meg nodded her head miserably. "I'm so sorry to take advantage of you like this, but I think something terrible is going to happen. What with the problems with the company, Daddy and Jay fighting—"

"Jay's back?"

"He's been working for us for almost a year."

Emma was shocked. Jay Cooper must have finally grown up if he'd taken on his responsibilities in the family company, although it sounded like he and his father still didn't agree on how to run things. "What about Frasier?"

"Frasier's the best thing that ever happened to me. He's solid and dependable. He never minds when I go off on one of my tangents. I'll admit I was a little surprised when he wanted to marry me, but I feel so safe when I'm with him that it really is the most logical thing to do."

No passionate declarations of love, no "I couldn't live without him," Emma noted, but she knew how false those sentiments could be. The one great love of her life had left her standing at the altar—literally. She'd gone down the aisle to check for herself that Max wasn't there. And, in front of a hundred guests, Emma had seen that her groom hadn't shown.

"I wish I'd had your instincts before my own wedding," she said brightly, knowing that the infamous day that had changed her life was why Meg had called her. A subtle but important part of Emma's advertising was her own story. How she had turned that day of betrayal and humiliation into a successful fund-raiser for the children's hospital was an ingenious promise to every nervous bride: that no matter what happened, Emma Delaney would save the day.

"I was in Europe when..." Meg trailed off delicately, giving Emma the choice as to whether or not she wanted to tell her sad tale.

"When I got jilted. It's okay," she added when Meg winced. "I accepted what happened a long time ago—on my wedding day, to be precise." Emma heard a note of bitterness in her voice and was surprised; she'd thought she wasn't bitter any longer. "I don't mind talking about it." She squeezed Meg's hand comfortingly. After college Meg had moved back home to New York. Emma had decided to remain in Philadelphia, accepting a job as publicist at a local art gallery. Then she'd met Max. Meg had never met Max. Few of her friends had, because their courtship had been such a whirlwind. And, of course, no one got to meet him at the wedding.

"How did you do it?"

"I was so hurt and betrayed that I had to do something or

I would have fallen apart. You see, what I never told anyone was that Max sent me a telegram. To the church." She closed her eyes and could see the impersonal, typewritten words: *Sorry, darling, but I can't marry you.*

"That's it? No explanation? No begging for forgiveness?"

"Nothing. Just that."

The two friends sat in silence. Finally Meg said, "That's just awful."

"Yes. And so I got angry. I had a hundred guests, a hall, food, a band—people were expecting a party, so I didn't disappoint. We drank and ate, and my friends came up to the microphone and told wedding horror stories. I sat up at the head table in my wedding dress with my grandmother and auctioned off the wedding gifts. All the money went to the local children's hospital."

"But how did that turn into your business?" Meg looked down at the napkin she was twisting between her fingers, and then at Emma, sympathy and horror in her face. "Doesn't being around weddings bother you?"

Emma answered the second question first. "Not at all. I love romance and weddings. I just want to make sure no bride has to go through the hell I went through." She fluffed her short blond hair with her fingers. Talking about her wedding did depress her a little, so she reminded herself that true love conquered all. "In those days, through my publicity work at that little art gallery, I had a number of reporter friends, who came to the wedding. Herman wrote a story on me—on how I had saved the day. After my two-week crying binge ended, I read the article and learned that I was something of a local celebrity. I'd unplugged my phone, so when I finally reconnected to the world, I found all the local morning shows begging me to come tell my story. It was a funny story, when I told it." Hilarious, indeed—being stood up in front of your grandmother and friends by the man you loved more than anything in the world. *Funny, ha, ha.* Then she shook off her gloom. Since she'd spoken to Meg, she'd been dwelling too much on what had happened to her so long ago. Most of the time, she pretended it no longer hurt, but every once in a while... "Anyway," she continued brightly, "I decided I had a golden opportunity. I'd already realized that being a publicist wasn't the career I wanted, so I wrote some clever copy for a brochure, used the photos of me in my wedding gown, and Have Wedding Dress, Will Travel was born." For Emma, the name of her business epitomized its purpose. She and her two assistants could handle any request. She had a twenty-four-hour emergency number and she and Beth and Susan had traveled across the country on a moment's notice to fix any number of weddings.

And every nervous bride, at some point, would ask about Emma's wedding, just as Megan had done. Emma would weave her tale, and the bride would be reassured that no matter what disasters struck, Emma could fix them. And nothing could be ever be as bad as what had happened to her.

Sometimes late at night Emma wondered why, with all the weddings she had been to, hers had been the only one where the groom hadn't shown.

"Tell me about your business," Meg asked, probably to distract Emma from her dark thoughts. Meg could still read her well.

So Emma told her about the shop—about the dresses she and her colleagues tracked down at estate sales, garage sales, going-out-of-business sales, from theaters at the closing of a show. "That's how we get some of the most marvelous bride and bridesmaid dresses we rent."

"Rent?"

"Well, you can buy the gown if you want—and some women do, for sentimental reasons—but since you wear it only one day, I like to offer rentals. Who are your bridesmaids?"

Meg turned a hopeful expression on her. "Will you be one?"

Emma was touched. "I'd be honored, but I should be behind the scenes organizing."

"Emma, please. I'd be very honored if you stood up with me."

"Then I'd be happy to. Who else?" *Always a bridesmaid...*

Stop it, Emma told herself. My, she was being morose today.

"I asked Sarah Tepper, from work. She's slim like you and a little taller."

"Everyone is taller than me." At five foot four, Emma had always wanted to be tall and willowy and elegant—much like Meg. Instead, she was short and cute, which she hated. Her platinum blond hair didn't help, either, nor did the fact that no matter what she tried to do with it, her hair insisted on fluffing around her face, making her look...sweet. She stretched her foot to discreetly check on the heel of her brown leather boots. Three inches. Good. "Coloring?"

Meg wrinkled her nose, "Medium, I guess, although Sarah's hair is dark. Well, you'll see tonight. She and Frasier are coming for dinner."

"So I'll get to meet this paragon of virtue who's completely knocked you off your feet?"

Megan picked up the coffee cups and placed them in the dishwasher, her back turned. Then she straightened, and Emma saw that she looked worried. "Were you totally and completely and head-over-heels in love with...what's his name?" she asked.

"Max. His name is Max. And yes, I was totally and completely head-over-heels in love with him."

"What about now?" Meg asked the question no one had dared ask, one Emma didn't ask herself.

"Part of me hates him. Part of me wonders what happened to him."

"You've never seen or heard from him in eight years?"

"No." Emma stood. She'd talked more about Max today than she had in a long time. She was tempted to ask Meg about her feelings for Frasier, but stopped herself. Meg had made up her own mind about what she wanted. There was a lot to be said for security and stability. For knowing your groom would show up on your wedding day. Although Emma did remember how Meg had once told her she longed for adventure. Was Frasier Meg's adventure? "Why don't we go to the library and get set up?" Emma said instead.

Meg led the way, and Emma was pleased to see all of her boxes had been carried in and set next to a large mahogany table. The garment bags had been laid flat on the flowered sofa. She'd begun to unzip the first bag when they both heard a car pull up.

"That'll be Frasier." Megan smiled. "I asked him to gather all the RSVPs my secretary was collecting, so we'd have some idea who was coming."

Emma shook her head. "Did your secretary really send out invitations to whomever he thought of?"

"Oh, no." Meg searched the back of her ear for a pencil, and not finding one, picked a pen off the desk. "I gave him lists, Daddy gave him lists."

"What about Frasier?"

"I don't know. He doesn't have any family."

"How did you two meet?"

"Why, at work." Meg looked surprised that there might be another place where people could meet. "I keep forgetting it's been so long since you and I really talked. Daddy hired him as vice president of finance and things just sort of developed." Meg blushed.

It was the first real sign of emotion Meg had shown over Frasier. Clearly she did love him. Not everyone expressed emotions as openly as Emma had for Max. Why, she'd fallen in love with him the day she'd met him and had told him so almost as quickly. After making love on the night of the first day they'd met, to be precise.

She hadn't been a virgin when she and Max had made love, but she might as well have been. His lovemaking had been fiery, passionate and explosive, like nothing she'd ever experienced before. She'd never felt more alive or more like a woman. From the first, she'd known he was the man for her.

Emma mentally shook herself and tried to work a zipper that was caught on a piece of lace. She had to stop thinking about Max. She hadn't seen him in eight years, and with luck, it would be at least another eight before she accidentally ran into him on a street somewhere. And if she was fortunate enough to be in a car, she'd be more than happy to run into him!

There, she got the piece of lace free from the zipper without ripping it just as she heard Meg exclaim, "Frasier," and rush over to him. Emma straightened and turned around to greet her friend's fiancé. At first she only saw Meg wrapped in the strong arms of a tall, dark-haired man. But then Meg moved out of his embrace and stood smiling at Emma.

For the second time in her life, Emma knew what it felt like to have her heart ripped out.

Meg beamed at Frasier. "Darling, I'd like you to meet an old friend who's going to help with the wedding. Emma Delaney."

Emma remembered the words on the telegram: *Sorry, darling, but I can't marry you.* She also recalled the wedding invitation: *the marriage of Emma Grace Delaney to Maxwell Frasier Thorne.*

In front of her stood the man she'd thought she'd never see again—Max Thorne.

He was about to marry one of her best friends.

And Emma was planning the lying, conniving bastard's wedding!

Mr. Right

MAXWELL FRASIER THORNE did the only thing he could do—
he extended his hand, wondering if Emma would take it or
kick him. Remembering her spirited nature, he rather
thought it would be the latter, but she shook his hand, then
whipped hers away. Other than the startled look in her eyes,
she restrained herself admirably well. He wondered when
she'd learned such control. If it had been because of him.

He'd taught himself control since he'd last seen her.

Megan was saying something about lists and caterers. He
realized he was still holding the large banker's box under
one arm, a box filled with names of people he didn't know
who'd been invited to their wedding.

His other wedding had been like that, too. Emma had been
so young she hadn't even questioned his lack of people to invite. Her sweet, white-haired grandmother had looked at
him questioningly, but knowing how head-over-heels in
love her granddaughter was, she hadn't said anything. He'd
seen the doubt in Mrs. Delaney's eyes, but she'd kept quiet.
He was glad he'd never had to face her after what he did to
Emma. This time, at least, he'd been able to put a few names
on a list so that he wouldn't be completely underrepresented
when he said, "I do."

But the last person in the world he'd expected to see at his
second wedding was the bride he'd abandoned at the first. If

there were celestial forces at work, he deserved this. But Megan didn't deserve it.

He knew he had hurt Emma very badly. He didn't imagine that she'd locked herself in her apartment for two weeks to cry over him, but she had loved him. Rather passionately at times. He felt heat seep into his cheeks and pushed his thoughts away from that direction.

Megan had taken the box, deposited it on the desk and was beginning to rifle through its contents. She looked so pretty with her soft brown hair curling around her face, the sunlight showing how calm and untroubled her expression was. He wanted it to stay that way. He also hoped she didn't get too caught up in trying to remember where she knew all these people from. If she did it would be days before she surfaced again. That was why he loved her—because she needed him. Megan might be a brilliant editor and a sophisticated woman, but she needed him to help her with the little details.

Megan Elizabeth Cooper needed him. And he was going to make sure that nothing made her unhappy.

So why hadn't he told her the truth about himself? his conscience demanded.

Even more importantly, why hadn't he taken over the details of the wedding after Megan had confessed to him that she had done absolutely nothing about the event? He'd been so immersed in the problems at Scorpion Books that he hadn't wanted to involve himself in all this female hoopla. His job was to show up and repeat after me.

Unlike last time.

Emma glared at him and then stormed over to the bay window, her rigid back to him. He knew she needed time to collect herself—she wasn't completely in control.

"Frasier, darling. Who are all these people?" Megan asked as she sank into a chair by the desk. "There must be hundreds of them."

"Four hundred and twenty-seven have said yes. We're still waiting to hear from thirty-three. I had Derrick begin organizing this morning." He should have taken charge long ago and then he could have escaped this mess. When Megan claimed she'd fixed the problem by asking an old girlfriend who ran a wedding service to help, he'd been relieved. Megan had even mentioned something about her friend having had a disastrous wedding.

It served him right for not taking charge. Megan needed him to help with the practical aspects of life. She got so caught up in her passions that she often forgot her obligations. He'd learned that passions only led to weakness. Passion had led him to Emma. Now his responsibility was to protect Meg.

Meg searched behind her ear for a pencil. "Four hundred and twenty-seven people. Thirty-three still to go! Oh, Emma, what are we going to do?" she asked in bewilderment. "Do you know that many people?" This question she directed at him.

That stopped Emma in her tracks. "Yes, Mr. Thorne. Do you have that many relatives?" she asked smoothly. Clearly she remembered his guest list eight years ago—of two people. "Perhaps you've made a lot of friends since moving to New York?"

Meg frowned as she rifled through the sheets covered with names. "Frasier's only been here six months. He can't have made that many friends, although he is very charming. But we can't fit 427 people into this house."

"Tents with heaters on the lawn," Emma announced firmly, and put her hands on Megan's shoulders reassuringly. "It looks daunting, but don't worry, we can work through it. After all, you've got the official bridal-disaster expert at your service." She looked straight at him, with a cold, disdainful sneer that he hadn't known she was capable of. "At least your groom will show up."

Inwardly he cringed, but he decided Emma deserved her pound of flesh. However, after an hour of sorting through guest lists and then menus while Emma kept up a running bitchy monologue on her wedding day, on her grandmother's stoic behavior and her friends' reactions, on what the bridesmaids did to the groom figurine on the cake—suffice it to say they had a lot more imagination than Lorena Bobbit—he was angry. At first he'd sat in a tense silence, wondering when Emma would expose him. Then he'd realized that Emma hadn't decided what to do about him—but she was determined to have her revenge. After another half hour of stories he was furious, while Megan was laughing so hard tears rolled down her cheeks. Now, they were reciting excuses the missing groom could have used.

"Amnesia."

"Abducted by aliens."

"Evil twin."

"Witness protection program."

"Oliver Stone was hot on his trail because he shot JFK."

"Oh, stop," Meg begged. "I have to go to the bathroom and fix my face. Then I'll get us some more coffee." She took his hand in hers and then Emma's in the other and squeezed. "That will give my old friend—" she smiled at Emma "—and my dear new friend—" she looked at him with love shining in her eyes "—a chance to get to know one another." He stood and watched his fiancée leave the room, a little afraid to face Emma alone.

The only thing he knew about Emma Delaney was that she had stayed in Philadelphia, where they had met and lived together. As a result, he'd kept away from the entire state of Pennsylvania.

Alone at last.

"Or maybe it was something the bride did that made the groom hit the high road," Emma said quietly, not looking at him. Instead, she busied herself alphabetizing the list.

"Maybe I squeezed the toothpaste from the middle instead of the bottom. Or heavens, maybe I couldn't make his favorite casserole just the way his mother did."

"Stop that," he said coldly. "It wasn't anything you did."

She raised a furious expression to him. "It certainly wasn't because I was the one who coerced him into getting married. I may have chased you in the beginning, but you're the one who begged me to marry you!"

That was part of another lifetime. Part of another man, a weaker man. Frasier Thorne no longer let himself be ruled solely by desires. He thrust himself out of his chair and paced. Stopping in front of Emma, he asked, "What are you going to tell Megan?"

"Nothing." Emma lowered her head and began to sort through the papers again. Her soft blond hair fluffed around her head. He remembered how she'd always tried to control it, but the second she got nervous she'd run her fingers through her locks, creating a messy halo around her face.

He pulled himself back to the present. Old memories should remain buried. "What do you mean, nothing? She's one of your best friends."

"Exactly, so I'm not going to do anything to hurt her. If you think she should know that you're the man who...didn't marry me, then you tell her." She slammed the papers on the table and rose so that their faces were only inches apart. "I only want to know one thing—do you love her?"

"Yes."

"Then that's settled," Emma sat back down, her face impassive. "Meg loves you, you love her."

"Yes, but what about you?"

"Don't imagine I've been pining for you for eight years! You hurt me but I got over it. I have a wonderful life now."

"Are you married?" He was surprised by the question. He could have found out the answer anytime during the past eight years, but he hadn't. Why did seeing Emma bring back so many emotions? And so many questions of what might have been?

Anger flashed over her face. "Not everyone has to be married to be happy. I've had lots of opportunities. I'm just a little...cautious over the process these days."

He winced.

"Don't think you're going to get away this time." Emma poked a finger at him. "I'm going to *personally* make sure you show up at the altar."

He didn't really know what to say—that this time, there would be no reason for him not to show? He dreaded her inevitable question: why?

Then he realized Emma wasn't going to ask. It was in the past and she no longer cared. He wished she would ask, although he still didn't know what he'd tell her.

Emma smoothed the papers she had crumpled into a little ball and resumed her study of them. He watched her check off names, the softness of her small hands belying their strength. He remembered all too well what they felt like on his skin, how quickly her touch could arouse him, and he drew in a sharp breath.

Eight years and she could still unsettle him. For his own piece of mind, it was a good thing they'd never married. His decision had been right, he reminded himself. Emma and he would only have made each other miserable.

"So we're just going to pretend we've never met before?" he asked her.

"Well, I don't really know you," she retorted. "Besides, it's up to you whether you want to start off a life with your new bride having a lie between you. If you'll excuse me, I'm going to go help Meg in the kitchen. She seems to have become much better in there since college."

He wouldn't know. He and Megan always ate at restaurants. He watched as Emma piled the papers together in what looked like a haphazard heap, but which he knew from past experience was a highly organized system. She could also whip up a gourmet meal for six from whatever was in the kitchen.

When she reached the door he called out to her. "Emma, I..."

She raised a brow, but he didn't finish. There really wasn't anything left to say.

"Tell me something," she asked softly, "Meg said you two hadn't had sex yet. She claimed you wanted an *old-fashioned* wedding night. That's sweet and so different from us." She smiled. "Or is it because you're afraid the sex wouldn't be nearly as good as with me?"

MAXWELL FRASIER THORNE restrained himself from hitting something as he calmly walked out of the house, drove the distance back to Manhattan and navigated the ever-present traffic. After parking in his private spot, he took the elevator to the twelfth floor, the corporate floor of Scorpion Books. All the while, Emma's taunt, *or is it because you're afraid the sex wouldn't be nearly as good as with me?* wouldn't leave his head. Her voice teased and scolded him—and made him remember. But he was no longer that weak man ruled by desires. Who didn't care who he hurt while he went after what he wanted. A man who had briefly believed that love would survive no matter what. No, now he was different. He even had a new name: Frasier Thorne.

At his office door, he greeted his secretary, Mrs. Kalin. She handed him a stack of messages and added, "Miss Cooper phoned to say you left before she could tell you that Mr. Cooper wants you to come to the house for dinner tonight."

"Tonight?" He suppressed his irritation. "Sorry, Mrs. Kalin, I didn't mean to snap. I just wasn't planning on driving back to Long Island today."

"Mr. Thorne, don't be ridiculous, you never snap at me. Young Mr. Cooper is waiting for you in your office." Mrs.

Kalin looked surprised, so he knew he must be scowling. The last thing he needed now was Jay Cooper and his problems.

He opened the door and stepped inside. Jay raised his handsome face from a manuscript. "Have you read Kathleen Drake's latest opus? So far the hero and heroine have had sex just about everywhere imaginable, and a few places I hadn't imagined! No wonder she sells so well for us. Where she comes up with some of this stuff I'll never know!"

"I leave the editorial side to your sister."

"Right, numbers are your game." Jay pushed a blond lock out of his eyes and gestured toward a pile of manila folders on the desk. "I've brought the files on the promotions for the last two years. Why are you digging through all this stuff?"

"I like to familiarize myself with the operations of a company."

"So you say, but there's something odd going on here. Why don't you tell me what it is?" When Thorne didn't answer, Jay shook his head, an angry scowl marring his perfect, classic features. "I know about you, Frasier. If you tell me the truth, I won't do anything to hurt you and Meg."

He held himself very still as he wondered about Jay's words. No, Jay couldn't know about his real job at Scorpion Books. Jay was only fishing. He suspected, but that was as far as it went.

"I love your sister."

Jay stood. "Father wants us all at the house for dinner tonight. More talk about the wedding." Unexpectedly, he smiled, his light blue eyes mischievous. "Did you meet Meg's friend Emma? I used to have the hots for her something bad when I was a kid. Does she still have it?"

Definitely, yes. She'll have it when she's ninety-two. He'd never even begun to understand what the word *lovemaking* meant until he'd made love to Emma. Once he'd touched her, kissed her, been one with her, he'd thought he'd never be able to stop. And what had he done after finding the woman of his dreams? He'd run away. The getaway groom.

Deciding to ignore his future brother-in-law, he picked up the files, rifling through them for the figures on cover print runs.

Jay took the hint and with the grace of a natural athlete strode to the door. "I'm bringing Sarah." Jay grinned. "Dinner should be fun."

Fun. Frasier didn't think so. He sat down in his chocolate brown leather chair behind his desk. *Max* wasn't running anywhere this time. *Max* wasn't packing one suitcase and creeping down the back stairs in the middle of the night. He owned furniture now, a whole living room suite, for God's sake. It had been seeing Emma that had awakened the old instinct. But he was a changed man. It had been a long time since he'd even thought of himself as Max.

Frasier was a man who lived up to his responsibilities. Who stayed.

He and Megan were getting married in less than two weeks. He loved her, he'd made a commitment to her—one he wasn't about to break.

In two weeks he was going to be a husband.

"EVERYONE'S COMING to dinner?" Emma asked weakly. She'd had about as much excitement and confusion as she could take for one day, and had hoped she'd be able to plead a headache and disappear to her room to think. But she couldn't disappoint Mr. Cooper. She had agreed to take one of the rooms in the Cooper mansion for the fortnight before the wedding. Meg planned to divide her time between her apartment in Manhattan and her old bedroom in her father's house.

Meg counted the guests on her fingers. "Daddy, Jay and Sarah. Jill Ellis, a new editor with Scorpion. The minister,

Reverend Ostley. You and me and Frasier, of course. Oh, I forgot Mrs. Daley, Daddy's secretary."

"At least I can ask Sarah about our dresses." The doorbell chimed and Emma realized the guests were beginning to arrive. As Meg left to answer the door, she stood up and paced the living room nervously, the pink skirt she'd changed into swirling around her legs. They had certainly cut back on staff since she'd stayed here last, but then she supposed that Mr. Cooper didn't need a lot of servants to look after just himself. Still, a grand old house like this one deserved looking after. Several times this afternoon she'd noticed neglect—corners that hadn't been swept, a tear in the fabric of the library's curtains. The windows could have used a good wash. She'd have to hire a full team of cleaners before the wedding.

At the click of heels along the hall's marble flooring, Emma turned around gratefully, eager to meet the famous Sarah Tepper. Meg had talked a lot about her new friend and colleague.

Jay Cooper entered first, his arms wide, pulling her to him. "Emma, you're as stunning as ever." The years had been kind to him, turning his boyish good looks into those of a mature man—a tall, very blond, athletic personification of a Ralph Lauren ad. He hugged her, a little too long for her liking.

When she finally squirmed he let go of her and laughed. "Sorry, that was for old times' sake."

"Stop manhandling the poor girl, Jay, and introduce me," an amused voice pronounced.

"Of course." Jay turned around with a flourish and said, "Emma Delaney, may I present the best editor Scorpion Books has ever hired, a woman of rare beauty and charm, Miss Sarah Tepper."

"You forgot about me," Meg complained.

"Scorpion Books never hired you, we inherited you."

Ignoring the squabbling siblings, Sarah stepped forward

and extended a well-manicured hand. Her grip was firm, and her brown eyes danced as she nodded toward Jay and Meg. "They never stop."

"It's traditional in some families."

"Must be a rich WASP thing. In my neighborhood we always stuck together in front of strangers."

"Emma is not a stranger," Meg insisted. "Why, she's my oldest friend."

"Jane Winters is your oldest friend. Her parents live two houses away—two Long Island houses away. Emma is your closest college friend, whom you haven't seen in three years," her brother clarified.

Meg swatted him. "I do better with words on the printed page than telephones."

"Don't I know it, child." Sarah flashed her beautiful teeth in a warm smile, and Emma began to like the sophisticated, dark-haired woman very much. Sarah took Emma's elbow and steered her toward the bar. "I believe we have drinks now. At least, that's how it's done in the movies."

"Stop that. This isn't a society event. We aren't rich," Meg complained.

"You are too!" Emma couldn't help her outburst, but sometimes Meg just wasn't any good at reality.

Jay was already at the bar, mixing some kind of interesting concoction. He offered a glass to Emma. "Long Island Iced Tea. Seems to suit the setting."

Emma took it and swallowed a gulp. Her nervousness was due to the wedding deadline—nothing to do with the groom.

Sarah turned to her. "Thank goodness Meg is a brilliant editor and marketer, because at times life just seems to be beyond her."

"Hey—"

"Don't I know it," Emma agreed, cutting off Meg's protest.

"When I asked her if our figures were at all alike, she said yes, except for the fact that you were a little taller than me."

"I'm five feet eleven," the willowy woman stated.

"I'm five four." They both turned despairing stares at Meg.

"And," Emma continued, "when I asked her if our coloring was similar, she said yes, but that you were a little darker than me."

"Honey," Sarah said to Meg, amusement lighting her intelligent face, "in case you haven't noticed, I'm black."

"Of course I've noticed," Meg said crossly. The doorbell rang again and she escaped.

Emma began to describe the bridesmaid dress she had in mind—a simple, sapphire blue sheath—to an enthusiastic Sarah. But then she felt *him* enter the room.

Max. No, *Frasier*—she had to remember to call him Frasier.

She had spent a miserable afternoon completely unable to decide what to do. Oh, she'd told Max—Frasier—that she wasn't about to blow his cover, but that had been in the heat of the moment.

He was standing with Megan and an older woman in an elegant red coatdress. Mrs. Jacqueline Daley, Emma remembered from her college visit. Mrs. Daley thanked Max for her drink and then surveyed the room. Meg smiled at something her fiancée said.

Emma couldn't tear her eyes away, until he looked up and saw her. *The sex wouldn't be nearly as good as with me.* What had she been thinking? The problem was that she hadn't been thinking but remembering....

Should she tell Meg?

Wasn't what had happened between her and Max Thorne old news? What difference did it make to Max and Meg's future?

The problem was all Emma's, wasn't it?

The problem was that she'd never found anyone she could

love as much as Max. Not even close. She tossed down the rest of her drink and faced the bar, holding out her glass for a refill. She'd spent the afternoon talking to Meg, and while she didn't think her friend was head over heels for Frasier, she clearly loved him. Thought he was good for her. Meg wasn't a child; she knew what she was doing.

So why hadn't Max told her about himself? Why was he using the name Frasier?

Why were Emma's palms sweating just being so close to him?

She took a large sip of her fresh drink. "You'd better slow down—you never had much tolerance for alcohol." She recognized his voice immediately, the deep resonance, the slight Midwestern accent.

"A great many things have changed about me over the last eight years, Mr. Thorne."

He was standing too close to her and she took an involuntary step back. He raised a brow and she willed herself not to reveal any of her conflicting emotions.

"I wanted to thank you for stepping in at the last minute to help with our plans."

"It's my job," she said coldly.

He stood awkwardly, looking at her. "I…"

She raised her eyes to his and for a minute he was caught, as if remembering everything—the first time she had kissed him, how she wrapped herself all over him when he slept.

"I don't want to hear it. You had eight years to tell me what happened. Now you and Meg have a future. I don't want to hurt her." Emma hadn't realized she'd made a decision until the words were out of her mouth. She felt the ease of a tightness within her that she hadn't even been aware of.

She had to admit it: over the years she had fantasized about running into Maxwell Thorne and extracting a slow, painful, cruel revenge.

But now that he was here before her, she didn't want to. That part of her life was over. She was over him.

Suddenly glad, she smiled at him. Before he could say anything more she turned her back on him, looking for Sarah. But Sarah and Jay were seated on the sofa, engrossed in a quiet conversation she didn't want to interrupt. The Reverend Ostley had arrived while Emma and Frasier were talking, and Meg had him in tow. Mrs. Daley was perusing the family pictures at the mantel and moved two. Next to her, Peter Cooper stood looking at the door expectantly.

All at once another woman rushed in, smiling at everyone as she made her apologies. "I'm so sorry, but I got held up in a meeting with the VP of sales."

This had to be the intriguing Jill Ellis, Emma thought, noticing how Meg's father beamed and made his way straight to her. Dressed in black velvet leggings and a royal blue silk tunic, the auburn-haired woman was more bohemian than Emma would have expected, but then opposites attracted. Still, she would have more easily pictured Mr. Cooper with a woman like the sophisticated Jacqueline Daley.

"Nothing serious, I hope?" he was asking Jill.

"The numbers were too low on D. C. Hatfield's book, but the VP's agreed to fix that."

"You can fix anything," Meg exclaimed. "Thank you. That book means a lot to me."

"It means a lot to all of us," Jill agreed. "We need to sell a lot of copies to make our spring list profitable. But I'm holding up dinner." She extended her arm to Peter. "Shall we?"

As the guests began to move toward the dining room, Frasier took hold of Emma's elbow to lead her in. At the contact of skin against skin, Emma felt a shock and her heart raced. "Oh," she murmured before she could help it. She glanced at Frasier, but his face was an impassive rock. It was only sexual chemistry, she scolded herself. She could get over it.

THE PROBLEM WAS no one had ever been as good a lover as Emma, Frasier noted sourly during dinner. Sex with Emma was part of the reason he hadn't taken Megan to bed.

Once he and Meg were bound to each other, he would completely forget about Emma. He would, he told himself again. It was simply a matter of mind over old, faded memories. Memories that were undoubtedly incorrect.

He loved Megan. They would make a good team. Their relationship made sense; there weren't any ridiculous ups and downs. No huge fights and passionate reconciliations. He and Meg were a mature, stable couple. They would grow and develop together. They'd be good parents.

His personal debate occupied his thoughts throughout the meal; afterward he couldn't remember anything he'd eaten. Meg and Jill had talked about books, while Emma had laughed at several of Jay's jokes. Frasier knew many questions were directed at him, but after giving a few distracted answers, he'd been politely ignored by the other guests. They probably thought he was nervous about the wedding.

The minister had spoken animatedly about the marriage ceremony, but Emma and Jill Ellis had contributed more to the subject than either he or Meg. At the end of the meal, Reverend Ostley excused himself, wanting to make an early night of it. The rest of the guests retired back to the library for coffee and liqueurs.

Meg squeezed Frasier's hand and smiled at him sympathetically, after he realized that Sarah had been asking him a question about the wedding. He blathered some response while telling himself to concentrate. He couldn't allow his confusion to become apparent.

Had Meg picked up on his conflicts? He hoped not. He wanted to make her happy.

One little touch of Emma Delaney's arm couldn't be allowed to interfere with his life. He'd just make sure he didn't spend too much time alone with her.

Emma laughed—her familiar beginning-from-the-toes, out-through-the-body laugh. Frasier froze and then slowly relaxed. Getting used to Emma again was just going to take a little concentration. He had faced a lot bigger obstacles in his life. In less than two weeks she'd be gone.

He watched Jill lead Emma toward a bookcase. "I can't believe you've never read Kathleen Drake. Let me find you a few of her novels. She's our biggest seller, plus she tells a damn fine story. I don't know what Scorpion Books would have done without her. She's our regular cash cow."

Megan sat next to Frasier on the brocade love seat. She smelled of wildflowers as she reached over and kissed his cheek. He put his arm around her and she leaned against him. He felt comfortable next to her. So what if his pulse didn't race as it had when he and Emma used to sit like this? Of course, he'd been unable to keep his hands off her. They'd rarely sat together *comfortably* for long; soon they always ended up wrapped in each other's arms.

"You're awfully quiet tonight," Meg said. "Are you worried about the wedding?"

"No, not at all. Meg, you have to know that marrying you is the smartest decision I've ever made."

Meg smiled. "Do you know, I used those exact same words about you to Emma this afternoon. It just goes to show how compatible we really are."

"Maybe Frasier's being so quiet because he's working on his alibi," Jay said. He slopped his drink as he put his glass on the coffee table, and Frasier was surprised by the frankly venomous look Meg's brother shot him.

The anger in the young man, his lack of control, reminded Frasier of what he'd been like. Before he'd changed.

Megan stiffened next to him, and he put an arm around her, wanting to comfort her. He knew that her brother was going to hurt her if he didn't stop feeling so sorry for himself, didn't start applying himself. Jay would also lose Sarah if he wasn't careful.

Meg stared at her brother. "Jay, you've had too much to drink."

"Not nearly enough to tell you what's been going on—"

"Don't be ridiculous, son," Peter Cooper smoothly interrupted. "But I do think Megan may be right—you have had too many cocktails tonight. It's not any way to impress Sarah."

"You can forget about driving me home." Sarah joined the group gathered by the fireplace.

"Don't patronize me." Jay glared at his father. "You think I don't know what's been going on, but I do. There's a thief at Scorpion Books—and Megan's about to marry him!"

The bachelor party

"HOW DARE YOU!" Megan was on her feet and advancing toward her brother. "How dare you try to ruin my happiness just because you can't decide what you want. I'm tired of you trying to blame me because of your indecisiveness."

Looking resolute, Jay raised his chin. "This isn't about who's the good daughter or the bad son. He—" Jay pointed at Frasier "—hasn't told you the real reason he's at Scorpion Books. And Father hasn't told either of us the truth about what's going on." Jay finished on a note of triumph as he glared at his father, but Peter Cooper only raised an eyebrow in return. Jay grabbed his glass of wine and drained it. "Nor has he mentioned a word about how he's had to take out a third mortgage on this house to pay for your wedding."

"Don't be ridiculous. Daddy would never..." When Meg saw the no-longer-composed expression on her father's face, she choked back a cry. "The wedding—it doesn't matter, but...is the company in bad trouble? I suspected something was wrong, but a third mortgage? How bad is it?"

Peter Cooper looked about the assembled group, at his son and daughter, his future son-in-law, his secretary, Jill, Emma and Sarah. He seemed to shrink in front of them as he admitted, "Scorpion's in serious trouble."

"But how can that be?" a bewildered Meg demanded. "We had five books on the *New York Times* list last year. And distribution has become much more efficient. We should be making more money this year."

"We're losing money in the paperbacks." Jay had moved to the sideboard and was uncorking a bottle of wine.

"Yes," his father agreed. "We're crediting more covers than we actually printed."

"What?" Megan stood in the middle of the room, looking alone and vulnerable. Frasier moved to her side and put an arm around her shoulders.

Sarah marched over to the bar and poured herself a drink from the bottle Jay had opened.

Emma was confused by everything they'd said, but she focused in on what seemed most important. "How can you credit more covers? What does that mean?"

Since the Coopers were busy glaring at each other, Frasier answered, "With mass market books—paperbacks—a bookstore returns the front cover of unsold books for credit. Whatever they paid us for the book they get back."

Emma thought for a moment. "You mean like the notice in front of books, 'If you have bought a book without a cover'...?"

"Exactly. Unsold books are meant to be destroyed, at which point the publisher pays the bookstore the price of the book."

"That doesn't seem very economical."

"That's a whole different issue, one any publisher can go on about for hours," Frasier agreed. "What's happening at Scorpion is that someone has access to our film—the mechanical mock-up of final art—and is printing covers, which are then returned."

"Oh." Emma let the facts settle in. "So, in theory, Scorpion could actually be refunding more books than it ever printed." When Frasier nodded, "It's just like printing money! But can't you figure out who's doing this? Isn't somebody returning more covers than you're expecting?"

"Unfortunately, large returns from wholesalers are the norm in this business. We can't risk accusing an innocent distributor—making a book distributor angry could mean an even greater loss of revenue if we lose their business."

"I'm afraid it has to be an inside job," Peter Cooper said.

"Daddy, you can't be serious," Meg exclaimed. "Why, everyone at Scorpion is like family!"

"Why didn't you tell us about it? Why have you been keeping a secret from your own family?" Jay demanded.

Pain crossed Peter Cooper's face. "I didn't want to worry you or Meg. I thought it would be a small problem that could be taken care of."

Meg couldn't bear to look at her father. She turned toward her brother once again. "It's just like you, Jay Cooper, to decide that anyone Daddy approves of has to be guilty."

Jay flushed, opened his mouth and then closed it again.

Everyone settled down a little, and then Emma noticed that they all slowly turned their attention to Frasier. She, too, remembered what Jay had claimed. But that was ridiculous. Maxwell Frasier Thorne had never been a thief.

Frasier stared at Jay. "I presume Jay did a background check on me, so his suspicions weren't completely unjustified." He looked around the group, then turned to Meg and took her hand in his. "You see, Megan, I'm sorry to tell you like this, but Jay was right to suspect me.

"I've been in prison for embezzlement."

AS EVERYONE GASPED and then broke into furious discussion, Emma escaped, heading to the garden for air. She didn't have the strength to deal with anyone else's reaction—not Jay's slightly tipsy, pleased look or Meg's shocked face.

As soon as the words had exited Frasier's mouth she'd known that was why he'd left her.

In the near dark, the bushes loomed at her as she walked around the fountain, but she lacked the energy to head farther away from the house. Instead she sat on the edge of the fountain and pulled her legs up onto the ledge. She spread her pink flowered skirt over her knees like she'd done when she was a kid and imagined what it would be like to be a grown-up lady and wear long skirts. Growing up hadn't been nearly as much fun as she'd imagined, at least not when it came to falling in love.

She'd been sitting there a long time when Frasier sat down next to her. "I'm sorry," he said.

"Don't say that."

"I am sorry."

"How is Meg?" Emma didn't think she could bear to talk about them, about herself and *Max*. She was afraid she might cry. If only...

"I explained what happened in my past as best I could. Right now she's helping Sarah pour coffee down Jay's throat."

"Does he always drink so much?"

"It's been increasing, especially the last few weeks. I guess he's known about the problems at Scorpion Books and has been waiting for his father to confide in him. It must have been even more difficult since Jay found out about my prison record."

Emma had kept her back to Frasier until this point. Now she swung around to face him. There was no moon; Frasier remained a shadow. "That was why—because of the..." She found it hard to say the words.

For a long moment Frasier was silent, as if deciding whether or not to finally tell her the truth. "After the bachelor party, I drove around. I don't know..." He shrugged. "I was excited—I didn't want to sleep. It was my last night of freedom. Unfortunately, I was pulled over for speeding and the cop saw bottles in the back seat, bottles someone from the party must have dumped there. I hadn't noticed them. Anyway, he took me to the station. Once they fingerprinted me, they had me—there was a warrant from the State of Montana for my arrest for embezzlement."

"How could you?" she demanded.

"I was greedy and stupid and didn't think I was really hurting anyone. The thefts were easy—McCord Industries, where I worked, left itself open in so many ways—so I took advantage. I didn't come from much and, at the time, money meant everything to me. Success. The good life." He shook his head, as though in disgust. "Afterward I felt guilty, but was too much of a coward to turn myself in. Ironically, prison helped me take responsibility for my mistakes."

"I meant," Emma said angrily, "how could you not contact me after you were jailed?"

"And ask you to wait for me?" Max responded bitterly.

"Yes."

"Don't be ridiculous. I had a crime to pay for. I was guilty." He grabbed her shoulders, and even in the near dark she could see him gazing fiercely at her. "There was no reason to ruin your life."

"How dare you make my choice for me? Or didn't you believe I'd support you?"

"I was guilty."

"I loved you."

"God, Emma, that was no reason to ruin your life. You were young."

"You should have trusted me, let me make my own decision."

He heard the pain in her words but tried to ignore it. He couldn't acknowledge how much it had hurt him to hurt Emma eight years ago. Or the fact that, surprisingly, it still hurt. He'd really believed he was completely over her. That if he one day saw her across the street he'd feel nothing except a faint regret for how things had worked out.

He'd never thought he'd feel the loss all over again.

And the desire that was just waiting to be lit. If he pulled her into his arms to comfort her, he knew the embers of passion would burst into flames.

He tried to make his voice as even as possible. "I was afraid you *would* wait for me, Emma. Lord, you fell in love with me without knowing anything about me. You believed every lie I told about myself, about my work. You never worried that my family wasn't coming to the wedding, that I had no close acquaintances."

"None of that mattered to me," she said quietly.

"I know." He sighed. "But I couldn't let you make the same mistakes I did. You were young, foolish and in love, but you had a chance for a better life without me."

"Prison must have been awful...." Emma's voice trailed off with unasked questions.

"It was, but it also taught me about becoming a man. A real man who worked for what he had. Who didn't seize any easy opportunity. Or take the love of a woman he didn't deserve." He shrugged. "I was lucky I got out early—after eight months—but I could have been there for eight years. And for eight years you would have been on hold. I wanted to give you a chance for a real life."

He ran out of breath, having said to her what he'd for so long wanted to say. Emma stayed quiet, hunched over, and he wondered what to do. He tentatively touched her on the shoulder, on bare skin that shouldn't feel so soft. She leaped to her feet. Clearly, he'd succeeded in his wishes. Eight years later she was repulsed by him.

Emma paced back and forth, muttering to herself. Twice she turned on him as if she was going to say something, but then began to pace again. He let her fume. Eventually she would run out of steam and realize that he'd been right. What he'd done had been the best thing for both of them.

Finally Emma stopped, placed her hands on her hips and glared at him. "How dare you decide what was best for my life? Maybe I would have decided that I didn't want to be married to a jailbird, but at least *I* would have made the decision. You're right, I didn't know much about you. I certainly didn't know you were such an arrogant, conceited, chauvinistic know-it-all!''

"Emma, you're becoming hysterical. Take some deep breaths."

"Don't you dare be condescending to me, Mr. I-Know-What's-Best-for-Everyone. If I want to be hysterical, I will be hysterical. I can be whatever I want."

He'd never seen her so mad, even after one of their infamous fights. Of course, in those days they'd had a much better way of making up. He stood up and reached out to still her pacing.

"Don't you dare touch me," Emma shouted at him.

She really was making herself sick with anger. He caught her arm and she froze. She looked at his large hand touching her slim arm and then into his eyes. He saw more determination and strength in her then he'd ever imagined her capable of.

"Let go of me."

He did, feeling a little embarrassed. He should get back into the house. Clearly Emma didn't understand what he'd done for her.

But he knew he'd done the right thing.

Emma continued to look at him, as if she couldn't understand who he was. Then her mood changed. "Max." She smiled at him, the devilish, teasing smile he remembered so well. She'd used it many times to seduce him.

His throat felt tight. "Yes?" Good, his voice sounded calm, reasonable. Very different from the way he felt with his blood racing through his body. *Control,* he reminded himself. This woman wasn't going to undo the work of the past eight years in one night.

She stepped closer to him and he smelled her perfume. Something exotic and musky. She put her arms on his shoulders and tilted her head to look at him. "You really believed you were doing the right thing by leaving me at the altar? Never contacting me, so I could begin a new life?" she asked sweetly.

He was glad that Emma finally understood. His own guilt had eaten away at him for so long, but now it was all right, because she finally knew that what he'd done was right. Standing so close to her, he didn't trust his voice, so he only nodded.

"Well, then I understand perfectly," Emma practically purred. "A big strong man like you knew what was best, while silly little me just couldn't think for herself."

Caught up in the scent of her perfume as he was, it took a second for Frasier to interpret what Emma was saying.

By then it was too late.

Emma shoved hard and he went toppling over backward into the fountain.

ONCE AGAIN EMMA FLED, this time back to the official dinner party from hell. Heavens, she couldn't believe she'd really pushed Max into the fountain, but he'd made her so mad! For the first time she was really glad she'd never married him, she'd never known him to be so controlling and arrogant. Deciding he knew what was best for her...

Men!

The group was still in the living room. While Jay had switched to coffee, everyone else held a drink in their hand.

Sarah Tepper smiled at Emma and made her way over to her. "Are you all right?" she asked, her bright brown eyes assessing her closely.

"Oh, y-yes," Emma stuttered. "The news was just such a shock."

"Yes." Sarah continued to study Emma.

Emma said nothing more, let her think what she might. The beautiful black woman was very observant and smart, but she could never suspect the truth. That she and Frasier had a past.

"Have you and Frasier met before?" Sarah asked, and Emma had a hard time not choking on the sip of wine she'd just taken. Damn, the woman was good. Clearly she had edited a great many mysteries and had learned all about underhanded interrogation techniques.

"No," she answered very calmly. "I've never met Frasier Thorne before." At least that was the truth—sort of. She didn't know this new man Max had become. "What made you think we'd met?"

"Just something about the way you looked at each other." Sarah moved her shoulders in the most elegant shrug Emma had witnessed and let her gaze fall on Meg's brother. "Sort of the way I probably look at Jay."

"He's clearly in love with you." Emma wondered what the problem was.

"He claims to be. But he's never made a commitment to anyone or anything for longer than six weeks. I don't trust him." Sarah shook her head. "And look what I've done to him. I tell him I don't believe him and I send him over the edge."

"Oh." Emma felt just awful for her. Jay was charming and handsome and witty, but would he make a good husband? Probably not. Sarah had a much more reasonable head on her shoulders than Emma ever had; she'd believed everything Frasier had told her. She'd imagined them like any of the great lovers in history: Romeo and Juliet, Anthony and Cleopatra. And look where that had gotten her. Eight years later he was beginning a new life and she was still stuck going over the same events again and again.

She felt movement as Frasier walked into the room. Conversation stopped as everyone's attention was caught by his soaking-wet state. Despite everything, Emma had to bite down hard on her lip to keep from smiling.

Meg jumped up and went to Frasier. "Darling, what in the world happened to you?"

"I fell into the fountain." His tone was calm, but Emma was glad he didn't look her way.

"How could you have done that? Oh, never mind." Meg touched his dripping shirt. "Jay, go get some towels."

Jay glared at Frasier and his sister, but then retreated.

Emma watched Meg fuss over Frasier and noted the soft way he looked at his fiancée. Caring and considerate of each other, they made a good couple. Unlike the famous lovers she'd just thought about, these two would have a happy ending.

"I think they'll be happy," Sarah said quietly to Emma. "They make a good team. You can imagine them together for a long time. You can see them old together."

"Yes," Emma agreed.

After Jay returned with towels and Frasier managed to dry himself off as well as he could, the talk returned to the trouble at Scorpion Books. Meg and Mrs. Daley tried to offer alternate theories, such as someone at the printing plant being involved, but Peter Cooper discounted the suggestions. He'd investigated every angle and decided the leak definitely came from within their company.

The group fell silent, but Emma saw everyone taking furtive looks at Frasier. He continued to drink his coffee as if unaware of five sets of eyes trained on his every move.

Really, Emma fumed to herself, these people were ridiculous. Imagining Frasier as the criminal was the most absurd thought imaginable. No one, not even Meg, said anything. Why wasn't she defending him? Emma had had enough. She opened her mouth and then shut it again. What could she say? *Frasier is such an honorable man that he stood me up the altar because he thought it was the right thing to do?*

And he did have a criminal record. For the first time Emma realized that Frasier had said he was guilty. In her surprise and anger, she hadn't really let his words sink in before. Surely he wouldn't have betrayed the Coopers by stealing from them?

She dismissed the idea almost as quickly as it entered her head. No, she knew Frasier. He might have made a foolish mistake in his youth, but not now. He was determined, responsible, caring. He would never hurt Meg or her family.

But he wasn't the same Frasier she remembered. The old *Max* would have been furious with Jay. And cold with Meg for not siding with him. For the first time, Emma realized how different this man was. So calm and controlled. So emotionless.

Mrs. Daley put down her sherry, her expression neutral. "Well, this certainly is an unusual evening. Tell me, Mr. Thorne, where did you work before Scorpion Books?"

"And did they suffer any major financial losses while you were there?" Jay added.

"Stop it!" Emma surprised herself by saying. "You've all decided that Frasier is guilty without any evidence. I can't believe you'd behave that way. Just because a man made a mistake in his past, which he's paid for, doesn't make him guilty this time."

"Emma is right," Jill stated. "We mustn't jump to conclusions."

"Of course you're right, Emma," Meg said. "We've all been behaving very badly toward Frasier, and I'd like to apologize to him on behalf of my family. We've been very rude."

Emma waited for her to say that she believed Frasier was innocent, but Meg sat back in her chair, clearly finished with what she had to say.

Emma heard herself saying the words. "I believe Frasier is innocent. And during my stay here I intend to help prove that," she found herself adding rashly as the startled group turned to her. Frasier's expression was furious. She was inordinately glad she'd provoked an emotion out of him.

Peter Cooper raised his hands. "We've had enough unpleasant talk for one evening. We came here to celebrate a wedding."

"My father is right." Meg rose to her feet and walked over to Frasier. She clasped his hand in hers. "Frasier and I couldn't be happier, and we're glad that you're all going to be part of the event." She kissed him on the cheek. Emma looked away.

"Emma and I were planning to spend the night here. Why don't the rest of you stay as well?" Meg offered. "It's awfully late to head back to Manhattan, and we have lots of rooms."

Sarah Tepper agreed, as did Jill Ellis, and then Mrs. Daley did, too. Peter Cooper led the trio off toward bedrooms. Jay walked toward the bar and picked up a bottle. He considered it, then shook his head and put the bottle back down, sticking his hands into his pockets. "Guess I've had enough of the demon spirits for one night. I'm going for a walk." He headed out the terrace doors.

"Be careful of the fountain," Frasier muttered, but Emma refused to look at him. She didn't want to be alone in the same room as the happy couple, so she wished them a quick good-night and hurried up the stairs to her own room.

In the Colonial-style white-and-green-flowered room, she leaned against the door, kicked off her shoes and rubbed her aching temple. It had to have been the absolutely longest day of her life. Frasier, Meg, Scorpion Books, Jay and Sarah—everything piled on top of her. Her spine weakened and she slid down the door to the floor.

She sighed and hung her head.

Get a grip, girl, she told herself. She could survive. It was only two weeks.

Her head pounded and she remembered that the Coopers kept headache pain pills in a cupboard in the kitchen. She got to her feet and opened her bedroom, to see Frasier and Meg disappear into Meg's bedroom.

Great, just great. Tonight was the night the happy pair had decided to break their celibacy.

Emma slammed her door shut, her anger making her headache recede.

It was going to be twelve days of sheer, unadulterated hell as she watched the man she was afraid she might still love marry another woman.

She was planning their wedding.

She was going to be a bridesmaid.

Emma really had made a wrong career choice!

4

You may kiss the bride....

"OH, FRASIER, I can't believe what went on tonight." Meg paced her bedroom. "The truth about..." She sank onto her overstuffed reading chair and held her head between her hands. His gut wrenched at how pitiful she looked. "It's just so awful."

He felt terrible for having hurt and betrayed her. He could fully understand how a successful, driven woman like Meg would be horrified to learn she was engaged to a criminal. He'd been planning to tell her about his past before the wedding, but he'd been looking for the right time. All right, to be honest, he'd ducked the opportunity on several occasions, never able to put into words what he should tell her.

Simply put, he'd been afraid.

Afraid he would lose Meg once he told her about himself. Afraid that Meg wouldn't believe he was a changed man. Afraid that if he lost her he wouldn't be strong enough to resist falling back on old traits. Old instincts that lured him even now.

Especially the temptation in the bedroom two doors away.

No, Meg was the woman who suited him. He liked the way she respected him and needed him. He'd doubted she would ever look at him the same way after she found out the truth. But still he had planned to tell her. Before the wedding, so she had the chance to change her mind. Now she knew. And he was very scared it was the end for them.

"Meg, I'm sorry you had to find out this way. It was unforgivable of me."

"Yes." Meg raised her face and flared at him. "How dare you not tell me? I can't believe you kept me in the dark about something so vital to me. To our future."

"I was afraid of what you would think of me."

She looked puzzled, as if not understanding his words. "Afraid of what I would think of you? Oh, you mean your criminal past." She waved that off. "The fact that you're a convicted felon isn't insignificant, but what's *important* is the trouble with Scorpion Books." She stopped. "That didn't come out right, either. Of course whatever hurt you in the past is important to me." She clasped his hands between hers, gazing at him with trust. "But I also know you, Frasier Thorne. You're a decent, honorable man."

"I was guilty of embezzlement," he said, wondering how he attracted women who had such faith in him when he didn't deserve it. He would prove himself worthy of Meg, he promised.

A flash of surprise and doubt crossed Meg's face at his words. "I'm not guilty of stealing from Scorpion Books," he added, wondering if he needed to tell her the real reason her father had hired him.

"I know that, Fraiser. But if you suspected something was wrong, why didn't you tell me? You know what Scorpion means to me."

He thought he finally did. Scorpion was the most important part of Meg's life. Well, he should be glad of that. He'd chosen Meg because she was so different from Emma. So why was he suddenly jealous? Why did he wish Meg would show the same outrage that Emma had expressed this evening at not being told the truth about him?

He pushed aside those traitorous thoughts, concentrating on this woman and this situation. "Yes, I know that Scorpion is vitally important to you. But I want to assure you that I have nothing to do with your father's company's troubles."

"Yes, Frasier, I believe you," Meg said with conviction. "But Daddy thinks it has to be one of us. Somebody who works for Scorpion. Somebody who has access to the cover film, which means everyone who was at the dinner tonight, except the minister, of course. Plus there are so many others—all the editors, the art directors, the production people. How can that be? Why would someone want to hurt us? What happens if we lose the company?"

"That won't happen." Max stepped toward her, opening his arms. Meg went into his embrace gratefully. He held her lithe body against him, running a hand up and down her slim back, and waited for his own body to react. Tonight might very well be a good time to end the self-imposed celibacy in their relationship. His attraction to Emma was proving that his nonsexual relationship with Meg was a stupid idea.

It felt as if he was holding the sister he didn't have, so he decided that they were both too stressed out and tired by the events and shocks of the evening. He didn't want his first lovemaking with Meg to be less than spectacular.

Was his concern for Meg or for himself? Both, he decided. Neither of them needed any ghosts from the past in their marriage bed. Well, to be honest, he'd be the one with the memories of Emma. Meg would be too worried about Scorpion Books to even notice.

Now he was being irrational, Frasier realized. Jealous about feelings Meg had for her family and its business. Feelings he shouldn't want to compete against.

He was always aware that a part of him had been relieved when he'd been jailed before his wedding to Emma. Even as the pain of his betrayal had eaten away at him, he'd also felt he'd been given a reprieve. He could never have lived up to

Emma's expectations. But he wouldn't let Meg down. They had a reasonable, sensible alliance.

Gently, he stepped away from her, but continued to hold her by her shoulders. "Meg, I'll understand if you don't want the wedding to go ahead."

"The wedding?" Meg looked at him, frowning, and then smiled in understanding. "Oh, that's a good idea. Maybe we should postpone it for a while, until this situation is resolved."

Ignoring the blow—had he really expected passionate declaration like Emma would have made?—he nodded. "I'll send out notices to the papers tomorrow about the end of our engagement."

"Frasier, no! I don't want to end our engagement. You're the best thing that has ever happened to me. Marrying you is the smartest decision I've ever made. It's like we're perfect for each other." Meg's face creased in puzzlement. "I see, you meant because of your criminal record you thought I'd no longer want to marry you."

"It's a good reason."

"No, it's not. For heaven's sake, Frasier, what kind of a woman do you think I am? What kind of an agreement do you think we have? I love you. Your past doesn't matter to me. What matters is the man you are now. I know you. You're loving and caring and responsible. You'll make a wonderful husband and father. Although I must admit, I do think you could have told me."

He felt humiliated at having betrayed her. "I agree. I kept waiting for the right time and...well, I think I was ashamed. I hated to admit what an idiot I was in the past."

"Well, then, that's all settled," Meg said happily, and kissed him lightly on the lips. "After all, I now know the deepest, darkest, worst secret you've been keeping from me. Most wives have to be married for years before they figure that out about their husbands!"

MEG DIDN'T EVEN BEGIN to comprehend the deepest, darkest, worst secret of his life, Frasier considered sourly as he stood in the corridor outside Emma's bedroom. What would Meg think if she knew that he was Emma's runaway groom?

He turned around to face Meg's room, telling himself to go back to her and spill his guts.

No, his rational side argued. Meg didn't need any more trouble, especially after what she had already learned about him tonight. She'd faced enough hard truths for one evening. She didn't need to know this last deep, dark secret now. But he would tell her. Tomorrow, at lunch, he promised himself. He wasn't going to continue with his charade any longer. He was going to tell her about why her father had hired him to investigate Scorpion Books, tell her what his real career was. And he was going to tell her about Emma.

No more keeping secrets.

But first he was going to confront the woman who was the source of all his troubles—Emma Delaney. The woman who'd haunted him for eight years was going to learn to control her impulsiveness.

Telling everyone—all of his prime suspects—that she believed he was innocent. That she was going to investigate and help prove his innocence!

He hadn't been innocent since the day he was born.

He knocked once and then turned the knob before Emma had a chance to answer. Standing next to the bed, dressed in a lacy, pale blue nightgown, she whirled around, surprise on her expressive face. Her blond hair was a frothy mess, as if she'd been running her hands through it.

"You!"

As he stood there gaping at her, unfortunately remembering her fondness for frilly, sexy nightdresses, she snapped, "Get in here and close the door before someone sees you."

He closed the door softly behind him and warily stepped to the center of the room. This might not have been such a good idea after all, he realized, recalling her impulsiveness earlier this evening.

"Well?" Emma asked, crossing her arms across her chest. He tried really hard not to notice how the action plumped up her breasts. Why hadn't he been so mesmerized by Meg's appearance in her bedroom? All he could think about was how close Emma's bed was. It would barely take three steps to have them both on it. *Just like old times. Stop it*, he told himself yet again.

"How could you behave so irresponsibly tonight?" he demanded.

Emma had the grace to look down. "I admit it was bad of me to push you into the fountain, but you were just so arrogant and masterful, thinking you were the one who knew best for everyone else, that...well, I lost my head."

"Not that. I meant claiming you were going to investigate the thefts and prove that I was innocent."

"I had to! No one else said a word in your defense. In fact, they were looking at you like you were the thief. I couldn't just stand by and let them accuse you by their silence."

"That's exactly what you should have done," he said through gritted teeth.

"No." She raised her chin, her eyes flashing. "And don't tell me what to do, Maxwell Frasier Thorne. You don't have any rights when it comes to me!"

"You could be putting yourself in danger," he insisted.

"That's silly. This is a white-collar crime."

"There's a lot of money involved. Money makes any situation dangerous."

"Then what about you? You could be in trouble, or do your professional credentials exonerate you?"

He froze. "What are you talking about?"

"Your investigation," she replied blandly. "Mr. Cooper hired you to figure out what's going on with his company, didn't he?"

"Yes," he admitted, knowing there was little point in lying. Once Emma was convinced she was right, she was tenacious. "How did you know? Did Mr. Cooper tell you?"

"Heavens, no. Of course you're investigating the financial shenanigans. Why else would you be working here?"

"I am the vice president of finance."

"That's your cover story, naturally. It may have been eight years, Max, but I still know you. You'd never be satisfied sitting behind a desk pushing paper. There's a part of you that longs for adventure and intrigue. That's probably why you became a criminal in the first place."

"Don't brush off my criminal career so lightly," he insisted, angry that she knew him so well. "What I did was reprehensible. I was weak."

"Yes," Emma agreed. "You have changed since I knew you."

"Yes. I honor my commitments."

"Like your decision to marry Meg?"

"That more than anything."

"Good. I thought you felt that way. I certainly didn't want to have to hire a bodyguard for you for the last week of your bachelor days!"

He returned to the subject Emma had left behind—how she knew he was a professional investigator. Ironically, his criminal credentials had proven to be a plus when it came to uncovering corporate crime. He ran a one-man operation, although he had contacts on both sides of the law that he could use whenever necessary. Moreover, he never advertised his services; referrals were made by word of mouth. Whenever a CEO realized there was something unorthodox going down in his company, he liked to refer to his network of associates first and to fix the problem without going to the authorities. Frasier Thorne got the job done very, very quietly.

Angrily he turned on Emma. "You just assumed that I'm investigating? That I'm a white-collar-crime specialist?"

"Well, of course. How else did you get your sentence reduced, if you didn't help the authorities with a case?"

"How did you know I had my sentence reduced?"

"You said you got out early." She looked at him quizzically. "What else could it mean?"

Since that was exactly what had happened, he didn't contradict her.

"I remember all those late nights when you were working on those strange computer programs. I never understood a damn thing you did but I always knew you were smart."

"You've been reading too many trashy novels."

"Isn't that exactly how it happened? How you got your sentence reduced?"

"Yes."

"See, I knew you'd turn out to be a good guy! And now I'll help you figure out what's going on at Scorpion Books. You'd be amazed at what people tell a wedding consultant." She grinned wickedly. "It's even better than being a hairdresser."

She was making everything far too easy. She had no real idea how weak a man could be. How taking the easy way—stealing—was appealing. Whoever the thief at Scorpion Books was, he or she could be very dangerous. "No," Frasier insisted. "You are not going anywhere near Scorpion Books. You are staying here and doing your job—planning my wedding." His mention of the wedding stopped them both for a moment.

"As I said earlier, *Max*, you don't have any say in what I do. And I am not going to stand by as everyone accuses you of being a thief."

"I am a thief."

She whirled on him passionately, her face ablaze with anger. "Not anymore. You've changed! You said so yourself. You're an honorable man! Even abandoning me at the altar was, in your opinion, a noble action."

"An honorable man. Is that what I am? You don't know me at all, even after everything!" He was furious. Angry at Emma for her pigheadedness. Angry at himself for feeling emotions for her that he didn't feel for Meg. He grabbed Emma by the shoulders and pulled her close to him. "Would an honorable man, one who's getting married in less than two weeks, do this?"

He crushed his lips against hers, determined to scare her, but the moment his mouth touched hers, he forgot his anger and remembered how it had been with Emma. How she gave generously, trusting him, wanting him. He gentled the force of his kiss, but not the passion. He wanted back every taste, every sigh, everything she had once been so willing to give him.

She opened her mouth to him and he invaded. He stroked her tongue with his and then caressed her bottom lip, remembering how she'd always enjoyed that, and she pressed herself even closer to him.

At the feel of her hips against his, he broke off, mesmerized by her flushed face and heavy-lidded eyes, telling himself not to sweep her up into his arms and carry her off to the big bed. Not to make love to her all night until they were both senseless.

"Would an honorable man do that?" he rasped. He stepped away, turned his back on her and left.

AFTER A NIGHT FILLED WITH too many dreams of Maxwell Frasier Thorne, Emma put on her swimsuit and decided a pre-breakfast workout was exactly what her frazzled nerves needed. She'd be able to clear out the cobwebs. Bring herself back to reality.

The little scene with Max—*Frasier* she told herself—had just been some weird *Star Trek* alternate-timeline experience.

In fact, it was almost to be expected.

She and he had a very significant history and no closure.

Yes, that was it, she assured herself, as she quietly slipped out of the house, not wanting to disturb anyone. Because of the Coopers' financial difficulties, at least there were few servants around to worry about. Well, to tell the truth, she didn't want to disturb Max—forget that silly name, Frasier. It didn't suit him at all, and she wasn't going to pretend that it did.

She and Max had been lovers, and they had almost gotten married. It was to be expected that some *old* lingering feelings and sparks remain. That was all last night's kiss had been. If Max had swept her up in his arms and carried her the three steps to her bed, she would have stopped him. At least, she thought she would have. She hoped she would have.

While she'd never want to betray Meg by sleeping with her fiancé, Emma also had to admit that some stupid, romantic part of herself had never forgotten Max. To others she pretended he was history. To herself she admitted the truth—she'd never gotten over him.

Her hopelessly romantic self had always believed she'd meet him again. And believed he'd have a good reason for having abandoned her.

She'd truly imagined that he might be part of the witness protection program. Even the truth—that he'd been imprisoned and hadn't wanted her to wait for him—made sense to her. It was noble in an idiotic kind of way. A male way.

She had also secretly believed, deep in her heart, that once they connected again, nothing would be able to keep them apart.

She was a silly romantic. She'd thought that true love could solve any problem, overcome any obstacle. She'd never imagined she'd find Max in love with another woman.

The truth hurt as she made herself face it, continuing her walk toward the pool. Her silly romantic heart had been waiting for Max to return to her life and to pick up where they'd left off. *She was such an idiot!*

Lost in her speculations as to what might have happened last night if Max hadn't shown self-restraint, she arrived at the pool before realizing someone else was already swimming laps. Emma didn't even have to study the broad shoulders, powerful arms and dark hair to know that it was Max.

Fate definitely wasn't on her side.

Deciding to ignore him, she dropped her robe and slipped into the water and began her swim. By the time she reached twenty of her fifty laps she had managed to empty her mind and was able to experience the feel of her body slicing through the water. At some point, she was aware that the swimmer beside her had left the water, but she kept going.

Finishing her routine, she climbed out of the pool to find Max holding out her robe. His brow was furrowed and he looked like he hadn't slept very well. At least that made two of them. "Thanks," she said, as she slipped into its warmth. "It's a little cool out here this morning."

"Yes. Emma, we have to talk. About last night..."

"I think the less we say about last night, the better. Except that it will never happen again."

Max nodded. "I love Meg very much. I can't deny that there's some leftover attraction between us—"

"Probably because of how it ended," Emma agreed. There was no need to say anything more. She did have her pride. "I have to admit that I've thought about you a lot over the years, because I never knew what happened. If we had just broken up, then seeing you again wouldn't have been so..."

"Cataclysmic?'

"I don't think I'd go that far, but certainly not so shocking. It's really no wonder what happened happened."

"Exactly," Max agreed. "We're adults and can make sure nothing like that...kiss happens again."

"Definitely," Emma said a little too brightly. "Piece of cake."

Max paced and then turned back to her. "I'd also like to apologize for yelling at you. I had no right to talk to you in such a manner. But you have to understand that you helping me with my investigation would only hinder me. I work alone."

Emma shook her head. Really, the man was as infuriating and stubborn as she remembered him. If they'd gotten married, they'd probably be divorced by now. If they hadn't killed each other first. Why, when she remembered some of their fights... She pulled herself out of remembering their fights, and how they made up. She was determined to help him. "Now that everyone at Scorpion knows about your jail time, people aren't going to be as willing to talk. They'll be watching you constantly and gossiping. No, you need me. I can be your extra set of eyes and ears."

"No."

"Yes. Your only other option is to reveal your real reason for working at the company, and then everyone will be even more on edge. And they'll feel betrayed by Peter Cooper." Emma studied Max. "You haven't told Meg that you're a...what do you call yourself?"

"The technical term would be forensic investigator."

"You haven't told Meg because there's another reason for the subterfuge as well, isn't there?"

Max sighed and raked his hand through his dark hair. Emma remembered that sign of frustration very well and realized she had won. She pressed ahead while she had the chance. "Who are your main suspects?"

"There are too many damn suspects for me to get close."

Emma sat down on one of the lawn chairs and patted the one next to her. His pacing was making her dizzy. "Tell me, that will help you sort them out."

Max flung himself on the offending chair. "Maybe it will

help to have a neutral third party hear my theories. First, there's Peter Cooper himself. I can't discount the idea that he's siphoning off the money for insurance. Publishing is always a risky business and Scorpion has lost as much money as it's made. He'd been trying to find an investor for over a year before the thefts began.''

"How do you know that?''

He sighed. "It's my job, remember? I've investigated anyone even remotely connected to the company. Too bad I didn't check out all of Meg's old college girlfriends," he added wryly, eliciting a chuckle from Emma.

"Too bad indeed. And I'm not that old.''

He looked at her and her heart begin to race. "No, you're not. You're still beautiful," he said softly, and raised his hand as if he was going to touch her face. Emma moved her head away and his hand dropped.

Max looked off into the distance for a moment. She waited for him to continue with his list of suspects and refused to notice how the few threads of silver in his dark hair made him even more handsome.

"It's possible that Peter Cooper may have plans to put the money back into the company via a silent partner after a great deal of publicity. Then there's Art Spiegle, the head of production. I've checked out his record and he's clean, but there's something about him that makes me suspicious.''

"You mean he's shifty?" Emma asked incredulously.

"Yes," Max said in an embarrassed tone of voice. "He's lying about something, I just haven't found out what. Jill Ellis is the new senior editor, and she started to work at the company just about the same time as the thefts began. Moreover, she seems to be the first woman Peter Cooper has been interested in since his wife died.''

"Who else?" Emma asked. "You can't suspect Meg?"

"No, not Meg. Clearly Scorpion is the most important thing in her life.''

Emma didn't interrupt, but she wondered at his statement. Surely he was the most important thing in Meg's life.

"No, I'm worried about Jay," he said finally.

"Jay?"

"He's my prime suspect. He gambles too much and has recently managed to pay off some really big debts. He drinks heavily and likes to live a lavish life-style on a publishing salary. Despite him being the owner's son, it doesn't add up. He can't afford the life he's living. Plus, he's always been the one who didn't fit in. Meg was the perfect daughter, never causing any trouble, the child who wanted to work in her father's company. Jay's held a lot of jobs and he's been fired from almost all of the them. Scorpion is his last chance. But he might be angry enough to want to hurt his father and his sister."

"I can't believe it's Jay." Emma shook her head. "He was always a little wild, but to hurt his father so much..." She stopped and raised her shocked face. "That's why your investigation is a secret. It's not *you* who suspects Jay. *Peter Cooper* is the one who thinks it's his son. Peter is afraid his son is stealing from him!"

5

The best made plans…

"WHAT A SURPRISE to find you two out here." Jay appeared on the pool deck from behind the cabana, looking at them very suspiciously. Or was it only her own guilt that made her think this? Emma wondered. She didn't have anything to be guilty of—yet.

"If I didn't know better I'd say you two were planning something," Jay continued, and Emma heard brittle anger in his voice. Did he know that Max was investigating him? That Peter Cooper feared his own son was betraying him?

"Of course we are," Emma answered brightly as Meg also joined them on the deck. Meg wore a bright pink, flowered wrap over a fuschia maillot and carried a large hat. In contrast, wrapped in a frumpy old robe and wearing a black exercise suit, Emma felt positively plain. As Meg leaned down and kissed Max, Emma realized with relief that the brother and sister hadn't overheard any of her and Max's quiet conversation. She did wonder what kind of a picture they had presented with their heads so close together. They'd only been discussing the investigation, she told herself. Moreover, they had agreed there was no more personal business left between them. "We were talking about the wedding."

Jay smiled grimly at her. "Is that what you two were *talking* about in your bedroom last night?"

"Jay, don't be so ridiculous," Meg said in exasperation. She sat down next to Max on his chair. He wrapped his arms around her and rested his chin on her head as she leaned back against him. "Frasier was with me last night."

Before Jay could say anything more, Meg continued, "About the wedding, Emma. After what we learned last night, about the finances and everything, maybe we should downscale."

"The guests have all been invited," Max reminded his bride. "I don't think we can *un*invite anyone, and we're going to have to feed them."

"Of course we are," Peter Cooper announced as he, too, arrived at the pool, with Jill Ellis. They were both smiling as if they'd... Well, Emma wasn't going to imagine it. She never imagined it about anyone over sixty. Jill stepped a little away from Peter, as if it was too obvious that they were a couple. Emma wondered what it was like to date the boss; surely in the office they had to be fairly discreet. She'd check it out when she was at Scorpion Books.

Peter turned to his daughter. "Darling, your wedding day is your special day and we're going to celebrate it accordingly. You've waited a long time for a man like Frasier to come into your life and you deserve him. I want my little girl to have the wedding of her dreams."

"But I never dreamed about weddings very much, Daddy," Meg responded.

"Nonsense, your mother would have wanted it," Peter Cooper insisted, and Meg stopped her protests. Lily Cooper had died while Meg was still a teenager, and Emma knew that they all still missed her. She was glad that Peter had finally found a nice woman he could love. Both Jay and Meg seemed to welcome Jill into their family. It looked like Peter finally had his happy ending. Except, of course, for the troubles surrounding his business.

Emma was rather glad when Peter's cellular phone chirped, interrupting this too-cozy gathering. More than feeling like she'd just entered a Katherine Hepburn-Cary

Grant movie, she was finding the underlying tensions too much to bear. She'd be glad to go back to Philadelphia and her busy, uncomplicated life.

She sighed. It also bothered her that she was the odd one out. Peter Cooper and Jill Ellis were clearly in love, as were Meg and Max. Jay and Sarah, too, were involved. Emma was beginning to acknowledge that her state of being single was no one's fault except her own. She had been pining for Max for over eight years. *Well, eight is enough,* she vowed. So much for her silly indulgences in romantic dreams. Max was never returning to her. From now on she would concentrate on the business of her business. Profits and future growth, not delicate lace and finely spun dreams. Spreadsheets and stock options, not imaging herself Guinevere to Lancelot.

And why did all of her romantic images suddenly have sad endings?

"Of course we're coming into the office, Mrs. Daley," Peter said into the phone. "I'm afraid none of us realized that you had left so early this morning. Well, yes, I guess someone from management does have to make a showing at nine a.m." He held the phone away from his ear and grimaced at the assembled company, then returned to his conversation. "I'll be right in."

He closed the cell phone and grinned at his guests. "Nothing like getting told off by your secretary." Despite his words, his tone was happy. Jill was good for him.

"I'm afraid Mrs. Daley is right, though," Jill said. "We are being irresponsible. It's almost eight o'clock." She yawned and looked sheepishly at the group. "Sorry, I've never been much of a morning person."

Meg jumped up. "Oh gosh, I have a breakfast meeting in town, and then a call with my TV writer. I don't know why anyone thought she could write a book!" She kissed Max on the cheek. "I've got to run. Can you drive me in?"

Max stood as well. "I'll pull the car up front in twenty minutes."

"Jill, I would be happy to escort you in," Peter gallantly offered.

Jill nodded. "Shame about the swim, though. The pool at my health club is always so crowded. And I pay enough for the membership that it would be nice to occasionally be able to use it."

As Emma watched the assembled group leave, she muttered, "Don't mind me. I'll just wait for my assistant to arrive."

If she knew her at all, the ever-efficient Beth would be here before 10:00 a.m.

She turned and realized one of them was still with her. Damn. Jay was frowning at the retreating Max and Meg. "I did see Frasier go into your room last night."

Emma decided to remain silent.

"I don't want my sister hurt." He turned on her, his blue eyes flashing. "She loves Frasier."

"I know she does. And he loves her, too. I would never hurt your sister, Jay."

He nodded and seemed to slump. "I believe that. You'll have to forgive me. I've been rather out of sorts lately, and with all the bad financial news about Scorpion, well, I've just been leaping to conclusions."

Emma decided to tackle what was bothering Jay. "I'm sure Sarah will come around. She's a wonderful woman."

"She's the most amazing, incredible person I've ever met, and I'm completely nuts about her. And for the first time in my life, being a Cooper isn't a good thing. Sarah knows all about my past behavior and she doesn't trust me for a minute."

"I'm sure you'll be able to convince her," Emma suggested softly.

"I'm going to prove to her that I'm good enough for her,"

he vowed. Then he smiled his wicked, little-boy smile. "I'd better head back to the office as well. Say hello to the aunts from Atlanta for me!"

"GARDENIAS AND PINK everywhere!"

"Champagne flowing out of the fountain. Are you sure we can't dress the men in Civil War uniforms? They would look so elegant."

As Emma steered the two petite, very blond aunts toward a couch in the family room and the waiting Beth, she silently promised herself that if one of the Coopers ever returned to their Long Island mansion, she would personally wrap her strong, capable hands around his or her neck and squeeze very, very hard.

"Of course, this foyer will never be as magnificent as the one at Tara," Daisy Winslow told her sister and the exhausted Emma and Beth, "but for a Northern house—" she sniffed at the word *Northern* "—it's tolerable."

"I think it's beautiful," Beth said loyally. "I believe your sister did much of the decorating herself."

The clever girl's mention of their dear sister appeased the women momentarily, and Beth offered tea. Emma recalled that Beth had a lot of aunts. Every year for months before Christmas she would spend hours making personal gifts for all of them—homemade jams, knitted slippers and embroidered shawls. Beth favored long skirts with tiny prints, hand-worked vests and white blouses. With her long red hair held back by a black ribbon, she had a ladylike look that pleased the aunts from Atlanta.

"Megan will be wearing a hoopskirt, won't she?" Primrose, the other sister, asked. Her hair was a slightly more unnatural blond than her sister's, and piled a little higher. Emma surmised that Primrose was the leader of the pair.

"I, er, no, I don't think Meg thought a hoopskirt to be very practical."

"Humph." Primrose huffed, and Emma experienced a wild image of the two Southern belles sniffing and huffing at everything north of the Mason-Dixon line. Primrose fixed Emma with an evil glare. "I do hope that at the very least the gown is white?"

"Definitely. Virginal white," Emma blurted out, looking to Beth for help. Beth, clever girl, sat quietly and shook her head, a tiny smile hovering around her lips that she hid with a quick sip of tea. Emma drew herself up to her full five feet four inches, but she wasn't able to tower over the high-heeled terrors. She couldn't imagine wearing a four-inch heel herself! She had to respect any woman who could.

"Great shoes," she said off the top of her head, and both Daisy and Primrose smiled at her.

"Perhaps you will put on a fine wedding," Daisy declared, and Primrose nodded.

"And I do need your help, ladies." Emma seized the moment. "Flowers. We'll need lots and lots of flowers, and the gardener seems to only work part-time." She'd learned that, while Phillip had retired, he still maintained his suite of rooms in the house and liked to putter around in the garden. "If you could help with the flowers and creating the perfect table decorations, we'd be so grateful. We have albums filled with examples...."

"And since flowers," Beth added, "are the symbol of happiness for the bride and groom, the appropriate choice is essential."

"Why of course, dear sweet child," Primrose responded, nodding to Beth. "Flowers are the centerpiece of any wedding!" She pulled at the peplum of her jacket and nodded at her sister. "Let us take charge."

As soon as the sisters headed out the balcony doors toward the gardens, Emma grabbed her purse, the keys to the minivan, and fled.

Let Beth have fun with the sisters this afternoon. Besides,

she was clearly better at it than Emma. *Coward,* Emma called herself. But she fled anyway. She'd owe Beth big-time.

She wanted to see Max and Meg together in what appeared to be their natural habitat—the office. She wanted to see Jay and Sarah and Jill and Peter Cooper. There were lots of romances flourishing at Scorpion Books and somehow Emma thought that was important.

Of course, it could also be the silly romantic in her. A trait she was determined to quash before this wedding was over.

SCORPION BOOKS WAS a tall, nondescript building near the corner of Broadway and Central Park that Emma walked past three times before she realized it was what she was looking for. That happened to her all the time in New York. Often the mundane facade of a building hid an unexpectedly spectacular inside.

The lobby was pink marble with vaulted archways. She knew that Peter Cooper had bought the building in the early fifties and that the property alone would be able to pay off all of Scorpion Books' debts. But she also knew he loved the company. Taking a small vanity press and turning it into a successful midsize publishing company was the second greatest achievement of his life. He always said his greatest achievement had been falling in love with Lily Winslow and convincing her to elope with him.

That the aunts from Atlanta hadn't spoken to them for years was an extra benefit, he always added with a twinkle. Emma wondered what Primrose and Daisy would think of Jill Ellis.

The walls were covered with the dust jackets of Peter Cooper's favorite books. From Meg, Emma knew that not all of the showcased books had proven popular or financially successful, but these were books Peter was most glad to have published. She recognized a couple of thrillers from writers she enjoyed. Walking along the wall toward the oval, futuristic-looking reception desk, she also saw several nonfiction titles about relationships. She vowed to buy the first on runaway grooms that she could find. Or a tome on curing incurable romantics.

"I'm Emma Delaney," she told the receptionist. "Meg is expecting me."

"The Bridal Consultant!" the young brunette exclaimed in capital letters. "Gosh, it must be great to have a job working on weddings. All we get around here are boring writers." She leaned forward conspiratorially. "I'm hoping my boyfriend will give me an engagement ring for Christmas." She held out a well-manicured hand just waiting for a diamond.

Emma was used to instant confidences from young women. Somehow the words *bridal consultant* held more weight with certain matrimony-minded women than the title president of the United States, so she began her wellhoned routine. "How long have you been dating?"

"Two years."

"How old are you?"

"Twenty-four."

"Then you're old enough to know your own mind," Emma agreed. She had been about the same age when she'd decided to marry Max. She hoped this young woman had more luck! "Have you taken him ring shopping?"

"Oh no, I'm just hoping..."

"It's fine to be romantic and to wait for him to realize that he'll be even happier as a married man, but men can be slow about such things. I know one young woman who waited seven years for a ring."

The receptionist nodded seriously. "You're right, Harry needs to figure out how much happier he'd be if only he were married. What do you suggest?"

"Take him to a mall and drop really broad hints. Then show your best girlfriend exactly what you want."

The receptionist considered Meg's advice. "He does have

very peculiar taste sometimes. I'll do what you suggested. Imagine meeting a real live bridal expert! Are you very expensive?" She blushed. "I mean, could I possibly afford you...?"

Emma pulled one of her cards out of her green leather purse. "Once you've set the date, give me a call. I'm sure we could work out some kind of reasonable consultation rate."

The girl beamed. "You must have the absolute best job in the whole world. I just love weddings!"

"So do I," Emma admitted. And she did. She loved the lace and satin of the gowns, the little flower girls in frilly dresses imagining their own weddings, the flowers and the rings. She loved the hopes of the bride and the groom. Their dreams for the future. She loved how families came together. Everyone might be scattered across the country, involved in busy jobs, but they all respected what a wedding stood for and returned for the ceremony. It was tradition.

A new beginning. Two separate people becoming one.

Just look at the aunts from Atlanta, who had seized the opportunity the wedding gave them to heal their rift with their sister's family.

Truly, there was nothing better than a wedding.

The young girl continued to look at her with awe. "Miss Cooper is so lucky. She has a great guy like Mr. Thorne, and now you!" She sighed with enthusiasm. "My name is Amy Severn."

Emma held out her hand and shook the girl's hand firmly. "It's a pleasure to meet you, Amy. And good luck with your boyfriend. If you need any more advice over the next few days, I'll be around."

Amy nodded, her dark pixie cut setting off her eager eyes. "Thank you! Miss Cooper's office is down the hall, third door on your left. A corner office," she added, pointing out Meg's favored position in the company hierarchy. "I'll call her and let her know you're on your way up. Take the elevator to the seventh floor."

Smiling once again at the power of the wedding consultant—there were few doors in corporate America closed to Emma Delaney—she made her way down the plush pink carpet, past pewter-colored walls to Meg's corner office. All the luxury and style that was missing at the Cooper home on Long Island was evident in the offices of Scorpion Books. Both Meg and her father loved Scorpion Books best.

Where did that put Max? Emma wondered, and then shook herself. Where Max fit into Meg's priorities shouldn't—*didn't*—matter to her. She was over him, she told herself firmly yet again. Or she would be soon. Max had made his choice. Clearly he preferred how he fit into Meg's life.

The famous Derrick was sitting at a desk outside Meg's office. Horn-rimmed glasses stood out on a thin face as he frowned at his computer screen.

Emma stopped in front of him. "I'm Emma Delaney."

"Thank God." He stood to shake her hand. His tweed jacket was too short for his long, thin arms. "I don't mind working as a secretary to get into an editorial position, but this wedding—" he shuddered "—it's a nightmare."

"That's all right. I'll take care of it now."

"You have my eternal gratitude. If you want anything while you're here, just ask. You can go straight in—she's expecting you." Derrick returned to frowning at his computer screen, and she heard him mutter something about the damn manuscript-tracking system.

The corner office offered a spectacular view of Central Park, as suited the future publisher of Scorpion Books. The decoration of Meg's office may have been in the control of a designer once upon a time, but Meg's many interests had clearly taken over. Emma noticed a photo of themselves as sorority sisters, pictures of Meg with her writers at different literary affairs, African tribal masks, movie posters, Native American art, a collection of teapots and a collection of Zane Grey novels.

And of course there were manuscripts everywhere. Emma shuddered at the clutter, but knew that her friend worked best in a jumble of projects. Meg was frowning over a computer printout. "Read any good books lately?" Emma asked.

"What?" Meg looked up and then smiled. "Oh, it's you." She stood, walked across the room to Emma and hugged her. "I'm sorry I haven't been able to spend as much time with you as I'd like. We haven't seen each other in years, you're planning my wedding and I'm still chained to my desk." Meg let go of her friend's hands and walked back into the center of her office. She picked up a pencil off her desk and began to tap it nervously against the side of her table. "The production department just delivered revised schedules and they've moved up all the editing deadlines a full month! I can't believe they did it. As if I needed this on top of everything else." She picked up the phone. "I'll just call Frasier and ask him to come here so we can discuss our plans in more detail."

Before Emma could object—and what logical reason did she have to object?—Meg made the call. Instead, Emma sat on the comfortable flowered couch, after she had moved aside the pile of books covering it. "The aunts from Atlanta have arrived."

Meg groaned and covered her face. "I'm so sorry to leave you with them, but with everything that's going on around here, well, I just chickened out."

"That's okay. I told them to go ahead and plan a theme for the wedding."

When Meg didn't say anything, but sat at her desk chair and began looking through a manuscript, Emma continued. "They thought a Scarlet and Rhett—together at last—theme would be good. You're not listening to me."

"Oh? No. I was just thinking about this book." Meg looked at her friend distractedly and then picked up the phone and frowned. "Hold on while I call this writer out in California. Whatever makes TV people think they can write books?"

Amused, Emma watched Meg make the call. No, her friend wasn't much different from college, when books and special projects had consumed her interests. Clearly Emma was going to have to plan this wedding by herself. And rather than worrying about Max showing up, she was going to have to keep on eye on Meg. The last thing she needed was for the bride to forget to show up for her own wedding!

Emma picked up one of the hardcovers from the couch. It was a medical thriller, and after reading the opening, she was quickly caught up in the story. It was only when she sensed *him* that Emma looked up.

Why did he still have to be so handsome? So tall and dark? The first time she'd seen him, she'd loved his strong face, his square jaw, a nose that was a trifle too long but that suited him. She'd always loved his nose. Dressed in an expensive suit with a white silk shirt and conservative tie, he looked even better than when he'd been hers.

Stop thinking like that!

He smiled at her and Emma's heart did a flip-flop. *Stop it. Stop it.*

"Neither of you noticed me come in." He looked at Meg, his brown-green eyes sparkling with amusement. "She's forgotten about us already, hasn't she?"

"Meg's talking to one of her writers and I started to flip through this book. It's very good," Emma offered weakly, wondering how one man could take up so much space in a room. She was having difficulty breathing.

"Once Meg gets on the phone with an author it's hard to get her off."

"She was focused like that in school, too."

They fell silent as the recollection of the past brought *other* memories to mind.

"But you have a deadline," Meg said, her voice growing increasingly frustrated. "I don't care if Steven Boccho is offering you a deal, we had a contract first." Meg tapped a pencil on her nose impatiently, held the receiver away from her ear and glared at it. She mouthed, *Damn TV people!* to them and then continued. "Tell me where you are in the story. Yes, that's good. Uh-huh. No ending? You can't decide how to end the story?" She listened for a moment. "Never mind. I'll catch the first plane out there and I'll be at your house by dinnertime. Order in something Californian and trendy and I'll read what you have." She hung up the phone and buzzed her secretary. "Derrick, get me on the first flight to Los Angeles."

"Meg," Emma said quietly, to remind her friend of her presence. "Meg," she said more loudly as Meg went to her office closet and pulled out what had to be an already packed suitcase. Emma was more than a little surprised that there were so many editorial crises that required immediate action. Then again, maybe Meg kept a packed suitcase so that on those occasions when she forgot she was going on a business trip, no one would know except herself. Yes, that was it. Emma would guess that Meg had a sort of weather-neutral assortment of clothes inside the black bag, perfect for when she forgot her trip to either California or London. Emma guessed that Meg had developed a method for working around her absentmindedness.

Emma stood in front of her friend, physically reminding her of her presence. "Meg, you can't go. We have a wedding to plan."

"I have to go. The book is due to production in two weeks and Zoe Dixon doesn't have an ending." She checked her watch. "If I can start reading and editing tonight, I should have a good sense of the project by tomorrow afternoon."

She turned around to reach for something on her desk. "Oh, hello, Frasier."

"Hello." He smiled at her and kissed her cheek. He picked up her bag. "Save the book, but promise me you'll only be gone for two days."

"Three days max. Oh, Frasier, you're so sweet to me. Zoe Dixon doesn't have an ending to her book and I suspect she hasn't written as much as she claims. And I know once Zoe gets on a roll, she's good. And it's so commercial, this book could be a real cash cow for Scorpion. I know I can sell it at Frankfurt and..." She trailed off, looking confused and dazed as she sat back on her chair. "I shouldn't leave now, should I? We're getting married in ten days. We have plans to make."

Emma started to agree vigorously, but Max frowned at her.

"And I should be helping Daddy with the company and the investigation...."

"Don't worry about the wedding. Emma and I can handle it. Can't we, Emma?" He looked at her warningly.

"Of course. We'll be fine," Emma was forced to agree as she watched Max reassure Meg. He crouched next to her and took both of her hands in his. He leaned his head close and whispered something that made Meg smile. Quelling the unexpected pain that stabbed her heart, Emma looked away and vowed to get herself a date for Meg and Max's wedding. Surely Jay could suggest someone.

"You go get the book we need. Emma will handle the wedding and I'll hold down the fort in the office."

"Mixed-up imagery, Thorne."

"I'm the numbers guy. You're the wordsmith." He pulled her out of the chair and handed her the brown satchel she used as a book bag. "You'd better hurry."

Meg cast a distracted look around. "Emma, I'm sorry, but I'll be back in a couple of days." She pecked Max on the cheek. "Don't walk me to the car or I'll realize what a mistake I'm making leaving you alone. People will think I'm a runaway bride." She chuckled weakly at her bad joke, then she threw her arms around Max and gave him a serious kiss. She fixed his tie and then looked him straight in the eye, as if searching for something. "Bye," she said quietly. Waving at Emma, she hurried off.

"Bye," said Emma weakly.

Max looked at his departing fiancée and then straightened his shoulders. *He really does love her,* Emma reminded herself. Max and Meg were so different from how Emma and Max had been, but that didn't mean they weren't in love. That they wouldn't be happy together. She had to learn to accept that and do her job. The sooner she did, the better it would be for everyone.

As Max started to walk out of the office, Emma called out to him, "Where do you think you're going?"

Max turned around reluctantly. "I have a department to run."

"I know. And an investigation. But even more important, we have a wedding to organize." She closed in on him.

"Together."

6

Kiss the bridesmaid...

TOGETHER.

He'd truly had been insane when he'd told Meg to fly to Los Angeles and leave him alone with Emma. His former fiancée had taken over Meg's apartment, stating it cut down on the commute from Long Island. She'd also appropriated Meg's office as her wedding headquarters, claiming it was easier for her to make the arrangements—with the caterers, florists, musicians and a multitude of others—from Manhattan rather than Long Island.

He could only watch in amazement as Meg's office became Emma's. The piles of manuscripts were giving way to swatches of cloth, menus and lists of romantic songs.

For the past several days he'd seen Emma and her assistant, a kind of hippie-looking girl named Beth, scurrying in and out of the building, often followed by dressmakers and an assortment of peculiar-looking men that he finally concluded had to be musicians. Several different menus had been served to Jill Ellis, Amy Severn, Mrs. Daley and various hungry members of the art department—what was quickly turning into the Emma Delaney fan club. He'd also been invited but had pretended to be busy every time.

All this meant Emma was too close.

He'd worked with Meg for over six months, become romantically involved with her almost from the start, and yet she'd never been a distraction. He and Meg had an easy, comfortable relationship.

He'd liked being able to drop into her office and ask how her day was going. Or discuss a problem he couldn't find the solution to. Or ask if she was free for dinner. He'd never had the almost irresistible urge to throw Meg down on his couch, tear off all her clothes and make love to her until they were too exhausted to do it again. And then drag her back to his apartment and keep her there.

But he had this urge with Emma. There was a small part of him that wanted to convince Emma to give him a second chance and to hell with the consequences.

No, that was the old Max. He'd decided long ago that marrying Emma would have been a mistake. The police had actually done him a favor by arresting him when they did. Eight years ago, he wouldn't have made anyone a good husband. Now he was a different man. A man who could be trusted, he told himself.

Unfortunately, with just a little over a week to go until his wedding, it was Emma he fantasized about. Who distracted him.

Her bright smile and easy laugh. The way she leaned in close when she spoke to him. Her fragrance. He always knew when she'd entered a room—he could recognize her footsteps, for heaven's sake. He wasn't surprised that she'd made a number of new friends among the people at Scorpion, her warm and open nature always attracted people to her. It was what had attracted him.

He remembered the night they'd met—at a showing of a young photographer's work at the art gallery where she'd been employed. He'd noticed her across the room, laughing and flirting with another man, and hadn't been able to take his eyes off her. She'd seen him, and at that first moment of eye contact, it was like what he'd been waiting for his entire life fell into place.

They'd met each other halfway across the room, but he couldn't remember much of what they'd said. Each of them had been trying to contribute to an appropriate amount of conversation before they could leave together.

As the first speech began, he'd taken her hand and she'd followed him out of the building. He'd brought his car into the city for the event, and they'd driven to his apartment in silence. Expectant, tense, waiting silence. Lord, he couldn't even remember if he'd asked her back to his place, it had just seemed so right that she would come.

Once he'd had her, he'd planned to never let her go.

And he remembered—everything. How much he had loved her, once. In another life. But the man who had loved Emma—Maxwell Thorne—no longer existed. He'd built a new life for himself. A life he wanted. A life he could control.

He was now *Frasier* Thorne, he reminded himself.

Meg fit into his new life.

After he and Meg walked down the aisle, after he figured out who was stealing money from Scorpion Books, he knew they would have a good life together. Meg wouldn't mind if he had to leave for extended periods of time because of work; she was a modern, independent woman more than capable of looking after herself. They would have a successful two-career marriage.

If he had any doubts over Meg understanding his career, her flying out to Los Angeles only days before their wedding eased them. No excited bridal jitters for Meg. She concentrated on what was most important to her: Scorpion Books.

So why did that depress him? It never had before Emma arrived on scene.

She was the one disturbing his equilibrium. Bringing up memories he'd rather forget.

Forget the night eight years ago when his stupidity and greed had caught up with him and taken away the best thing he'd every had. That he would ever have.

He remembered holding the phone in his hand at the police station and dialing Emma's number. He knew she'd come to his rescue and that she'd forgive him. Instead, trying to do the right thing for once in his life, he'd hung up after the first ring. And sent her that cold, unfeeling telegram claiming he didn't really love her. That the possibility of spending a lifetime together wasn't what he wanted more than anything.

Damn, that had hurt. Not only losing Emma, but letting her believe that he hadn't loved her enough. He'd loved her too much to let her waste her life on a man like him.

And he'd been right. She'd recovered amazingly quickly from his betrayal, if how she had responded to his no-show was any indication. She'd turned her own wedding fiasco into an incredibly successful business. Over the past few days he'd checked up on her and learned that she'd recently turned down an offer to franchise her company, insisting that it was the personal touch that made her enterprise such a success.

She was right. It was her passion, her caring and her obvious concern that her clients responded to, that made Have Wedding Dress, Will Travel an extremely profitable and well-run business. His contacts had only investigated her professional life, however.

But he knew.

A loving and passionate woman like Emma would never be alone. Back in Philadelphia she probably had a long list of suitors. But once any man had made love to Emma, had kissed her sweet mouth, caressed her delightful body, how could he let her go? He also remembered the thrill of being seduced by Emma. How she had once met him after one of his late meetings, wearing a short, belted raincoat, a wicked smile and nothing else. They had made it only as far as a supply cupboard before he'd pulled her in, unbelted her coat and learned she really was naked—and just as desperate for him as he was for her.... He pulled himself out of those dangerous remembrances.

So why wasn't she married? He frowned. Emma should be married, not only because it would make their present situation so much easier.

He loved Meg, he told himself. If Emma was in love as well, there would be no problem. No brushing of hands and sudden pulling back. No staring at her until she noticed and blushed. No wondering what they would have been like eight years later if he hadn't destroyed their future.

No, he decided. It seemed that Emma was determined to devil him. To make him suffer now for what he'd put her through then.

And now she was missing. He'd gone to her office, to Meg's office, but other than almost being knocked over by Beth, who was racing out to meet the aunts, he'd found no one there. Beth had merely shrugged when he asked.

Well, Emma had to be here somewhere. There was a curious kind of energy around Scorpion Books whenever she was within its walls, and he could sense it now. He walked over to the reception desk and waited for Amy to finish flipping through a bridal magazine. Finally she noticed him, blushed and tried to hide the magazine.

"It's okay, Amy. Half the female population of our company has caught wedding fever."

"You're being patronizing, Mr. Thorne. Art Spiegle has also been very interested in Ms. Delaney's plans. It's only natural to want to consult with an authority if the opportunity arises. I seem to remember a lot of men, yourself included, fawning over a certain basketball player when he came here for a meeting." Amy raised her chin and stared defiantly at him.

"You're right, Amy. I'm afraid with everyone so occupied with the details of my wedding, I'm more than a little nervous. And a little quick to criticize." And remembering far too much of the past. Especially the sex. Which was only because he hadn't taken Meg to bed. But he planned to rectify that the moment she arrived back in New York.

"You're forgiven," Amy said. "Was there something you wanted?"

"Yes. Have you seen Ms. Delaney?"

"Not since Beth brought in the wedding cake."

"A wedding cake?"

"Yes. It's fabulous. I don't think I've ever seen such a large one, except maybe in the movies." Amy sighed as Max wondered why on earth a large wedding cake had been delivered to the office. Even he knew that the cake would grow stale before the wedding eight days away.

"Where would the wedding cake be?"

"Next to the coffee machine in the art-production area." As he thanked her, Amy turned back to her wedding magazine.

Indeed, in the small cubbyhole that art and production services had foraged for themselves—he believed it had once been a storage room for art supplies—he stopped and stared in amazement. He had always been generally aware that there was a coffee-gossip room to which upper management was not invited, and he'd always known where it was, but he'd never actually been in it before.

The twenty-by-ten area didn't look like it belonged in a large corporation, but like a real coffee shop visited by artists. That's the only way he could describe it. From the cheery yellow walls, the one pink chair, the vivid blue-yellow-and-green sofa, from the multitude of artifacts on the walls, several mirrors with elaborate frames and homemade bead lampshades, it looked like a place where everyone had contributed some small part.

Pushed into the corner on a rolling cart was a large cake. His wedding cake? Pink with white roses all over it, the cake was just the kind of romantic confection that Emma would choose. His former fiancée, his temptation, sat next to the cake, her files spread on the sofa next to her. "Cake?" she asked, raising her head. "Oh, it's you."

"Don't I get cake?" he asked ridiculously.

"The cake is really a bribe. I'm investigating. I've found that people spill all kinds of details when plied with sugar. Although I think you're more of a savory man...?"

He'd like to savor those full lips, which curved in a wicked smile. He'd kiss her until her breath caught and all amusement fled from her eyes, to be replaced by desire.... "What are you investigating?" he blurted out.

"The thefts at Scorpion Books, of course." She looked at him so innocently his hands twitched. Instead, he put some distance between them.

"Investigating? My job," he whispered furiously, so no one could overhear them, "is to run this investigation. Yours is to plan my wedding. And that's it."

"But have you learned anything?"

"Yes."

She looked at him expectantly, but he wasn't going to say anything about the cover approvals that Jay had signed. Covers that were part of the suspect group of large returns. He'd just gotten to the old files, and there was Jay's signature all over them. Would Jay really have been that careless? It could have been one of his early endeavors, before he learned to cover his tracks better, or to worry that someone might be suspicious. Max was going to keep this new, incriminating information to himself, however. It would break Peter Cooper's heart if Jay really was the guilty party. Max wanted to make sure he was right before he presented the evidence.

Unfortunately, knowing human nature, including his own, he was growing more and more convinced that Jay was the guilty party.

And now Emma was playing spy. He'd always admired

her gung-ho attitude, her willingness to try anything, but this foolish spiritedness could get her into trouble. What if Jay, or whoever it was, became suspicious of Emma's questions? She might believe that a few innocent queries couldn't hurt her, but he knew better. So far several hundred thousand dollars had been stolen. He'd gone to jail for less. Others had been killed for less.

"We need to talk." He grabbed her arm and started to pull her along the corridor toward her office.

"Max, what the—"

"Frasier!" He turned around once to glare at her.

Emma kept her mouth shut until they entered Meg's office. He was so angry at her, he had to sit down to catch his breath. He scowled at her, but Emma refused to be intimidated by his dark mood. Instead she walked to the desk and picked up several boxes. He got out of his chair and grabbed the precariously piled boxes out of Emma's arms. She smiled at him gratefully. Reminding himself to breathe, he grumbled, "This wedding is taking more planning than a military campaign."

"That's because most generals only have the enemy to worry about. They don't have the aunts from Atlanta."

"How are they?"

"I've left them to do the calligraphy on the place cards and the menus. As long as they're busy, Daisy and Primrose are just fine. Luckily, Beth has a real talent for making them believe her ideas are their ideas. The aunts want to be helpful, they're just a little used to having their own way."

"Stalin was used to having things his own way. The aunts are *determined* to have things their own way." He shuddered. "They wanted me to wear a Confederate uniform for the wedding—and I've never even vacationed in Florida, much less spent much time in any of the Southern states."

"No, really, they're very sweet," Emma insisted. "I think they regret all the years they were mad at their sister for marrying Mr. Cooper, regret cutting themselves off from her and the children. In their own way they're trying to make amends." She looked at him squarely, an inquisitive expression on her face. "They want the wedding to be perfect. They want Meg to be happy."

"That's what I want, too," he said gruffly. How awkward, explaining his relationship to Emma. But he felt he owed her. Moreover, she knew him better than almost anyone. She would understand. Naturally, Emma was more than a little curious about how he and Meg had fallen in love, and he knew that she would dig until she found out. He wanted to tell her.

He pointed to a chair and sat down himself. Emma took a deep breath, as if she knew what he was going to say.

"I owe you an explanation," he said. "And once I've told you everything, you can leave me to do my job. And you can do yours."

Emma didn't say anything, merely looked at him questioningly.

"I asked Meg out for dinner to learn more about Scorpion Books," he began. "Peter Cooper knows his business and the numbers, but Meg knows the people. She's good at sensing mood and underlying tensions. By the end of the first evening I knew I wanted to see more of her because I liked her." He stopped, unsure how to put into words what he had felt for Meg, what he still experienced whenever he was around her. Why he wanted to marry her. "She felt so comfortable. It was like we'd been lifelong friends and I could tell her anything."

Emma refrained from pointing out that he hadn't told Meg everything. He continued. "Her father had sworn me to secrecy about Scorpion Books—not because he ever worried about Meg, but..."

"Because of Jay. And how transparent Meg would be in her concern over him and her worry for the company."

"Yes."

Max stood and paced the room, stopping to look at the view of Central Park. "I wanted to tell her about my past—about prison, about you. I never imagined the two of you were friends, but I wanted her to know what I had done. How I had hurt you. I had it all planned out one evening. Before I could think how to begin, I heard myself asking her to marry me. She said yes and I couldn't bear to disillusion her."

He ran a hand through his hair. "I don't know, it's kind of as if she saw me as her hero. I couldn't ruin that so quickly. And I wanted time to woo her—"

"As you never had me?"

"Yes." He looked at Emma in dawning realization. "Much of my relationship with Meg has been exactly opposite to how we were involved."

"Were you never serious about anyone other than Meg?" Emma seemed surprised at her own question, and before he could answer, she hurried on. "So Meg is the opposite of me and she's the perfect woman for you."

"It's not like that, Emma. None of this was deliberate. But I did make so many mistakes with you. With us."

"The worst was never telling me what happened!"

"No, the most horrible was becoming the kind of man who would steal and still think he could be your husband."

"I would have waited for you. I loved you."

Emma's emotions were so plain on her face that he felt like he'd been punched in the gut. No, Emma was only remembering old feelings; she'd been over him a long time. She no longer loved him. He tried to tell her what it had been like. "I loved you, too. I knew you would have waited for me, but I didn't deserve you."

Emma turned away from him and he had to stop himself from going over to her and pulling her into his arms. *Only to comfort her*, he told himself.

"I never knew who my father was," Max continued. He might as well tell her everything. "He disappeared as soon as my mother told him she was pregnant. She struggled and did the best she could, and we got along. She loved me and always told me I was the best. That I could be whatever I wanted to be. I think I believed her a little too much. Luckily, I was smart and loved computers, so I got a college scholarship. But once I was at Duke I became envious." This part was difficult to admit. "All the rich kids had everything given to them, including a sports car and a job after graduation. I wanted a life like that. The good life. Nice things."

He stopped for a minute, realizing he was embarrassed at what he had to say next. "Mom had a brother. Uncle Nick helped her a lot when I was a kid. He'd drift in and out of our lives, but I worshiped him. He was handsome and charming, always immaculately dressed, always had a new car. And women. And money. He'd stay with us for a week or two and then he'd be gone in the middle of the night."

Frasier let himself get caught up in his memories. "When I was twelve I began working for Uncle Nick—helping with whatever scam he'd dreamed up. Sometimes I pretended to be hit by a car, and Uncle Nick would rush to my rescue, telling the distraught driver we didn't have any health insurance. He'd convince them to pay him. Other times he sold fake insurance or time shares—having a kid with him made it all seem more legitimate.

"I loved it. All of it. The excitement. I loved the stupidity of the people we scammed. I thought we were so much better and smarter than them. I even loved it when Uncle Nick disappeared because the game had gotten too hot. I never knew what would happen the next day.

"When I was in high school, Uncle Nick seemed to disappear for good, and I didn't think much about our activities or how they had influenced me." He was almost too ashamed to say the rest. "I liked college and after school I got a job—a legitimate job with McCord Industries. I worked hard for Jack McCord and watched his family members and friends get ahead without doing half the work I did. I grew bitter. I'd never thought about following Uncle Nick's footsteps, but suddenly I was doing it."

Max glanced at Emma briefly, then had to look away. "It was so easy. I took a little at first, then a little more, and covered my tracks. I could probably still be stealing from them if the IRS hadn't done a surprise audit. When I found out, I pretended I was taking a long overdue vacation and left. It was weeks before Jack figured out I wasn't coming back. Even then he wouldn't believe it was me who had stolen from him."

"How do you know that?"

"He visited me in jail. He was a lot more forgiving and magnanimous than I could ever have been. I've learned from him. He helped me to become who I am now."

"A man who lives up to his commitments. A man who's in love with Meg."

"Yes." He walked over to her and sat down on the couch next to her, taking her hands in his. She looked funny, as if she was lost in a memory, and he recalled how he used to hold her close to him, how he sometimes framed her face with his hands so he could watch her expression as he joined his body with hers.

"Stop that," he said harshly, dropping her hands.

"What?"

"You were thinking...about us."

Mortified, Emma dropped her gaze to her hands, now clasped on her lap. "You could always read my face," she said, remembering.

"Only because you telegraph everything so clearly. You never taught yourself to hide your feelings or keep secrets."

"And you learned how to read people like me." Then her

voice grew angry. He'd never heard her quite this angry before. "I was only thinking about sex."

Max grimaced. He looked at her, looked away and then looked again. "Don't think about sex, especially not between us."

"I don't want to! But it's not easy to forget."

He took her hand again, then dropped it as if he'd been jolted by electricity. "Emma, we should stay away from each other."

"Max, if there was nothing between us you wouldn't have such a hard time being in the same room with me. Are you sure you really love Meg?"

"Yes, dammit!" He struck the coffee table with his hand, furious at her. At this situation. He shouldn't be dealing with Emma just before his wedding. *Especially* before his wedding.

Emma picked up her files. "Well then, fine. Everything's all right. I'll try to stay out of your way, but we do have plans to arrange. Normally I like to consult with both bride and groom, but since Meg isn't here I need your input."

He didn't look at her. "Whatever you think is best is what you should do."

"No. This is your wedding. I need you to decide." She grabbed a notebook, flipped it open and announced, "You can have one of three kinds of cake within the budget we've established—traditional white cake, chocolate cake or carrot cake." He looked at her, puzzled, unable to believe he was supposed to worry about details like that.

"Carrot," he guessed.

She began to write it down, but then looked up at him. "When we were in college, Meg hated carrot cake. Has she changed since then...?" She trailed off delicately.

"No. I don't know. Make it traditional."

"Traditional seems to be a theme with you. No sex. White cake."

"You're pushing me too far, Emma." He'd grabbed her shoulders; he didn't even remember moving toward her. She raised her chin, her eyes clashing with his, glaring at him. They were both breathing hard and he could imagine what it would be like to taste her.

"I dare you," she whispered.

"I told you not to push me."

"I don't do what you tell me to do—anymore. That was over a long time ago. Come on, *Max*, prove that there's nothing between us except a little bit of old chemistry." She wrapped her fist around his tie and pulled him even closer to her, so close that he felt her breath as she whispered, "I dare you."

He fell on her as if toppled by a cosmic force. He crushed his lips over hers and pressed his body on her, pushing her down on the couch like a conqueror. But that was a delusion, for the first touch of her tongue along his lips made him her slave.

He had no idea what he was doing except that he had to touch or feel as much of Emma as possible. She'd opened her mouth to him and he took possession. There was no need for gentle exploration and teasing; they were lovers who remembered what the firestorm could be like between them, and they were entering its fiery path willingly.

He angled his mouth the way he knew she liked it, and heard her moan. Pulling her lower lip into his mouth, he nibbled and sucked, dragging her further along into the madness. When he filled his hands with her breasts, she gasped and he ripped open the top buttons of her blouse. Emma's lips were on his neck and she gasped again as his thumbs rubbed over her nipples.

"Max, stop," she whispered into his ear.

"Too late," he growled, and laved the valley between her breasts. She shuddered, then tried to push him away.

"Max," she said rather desperately. "Stop! Someone's at the door."

Slowly her words sunk in. He raised his head, trying to remember where he was, who he was. He was Frasier Thorne, groom-to-be in eight days. So what was he doing making love to the wrong bride?

Something borrowed...

"NO, FRASIER, I'm afraid I won't be able to come home to-day." Meg sounded very far away to him, as if she was concentrating on something else.

"You have to," he said. *Or else I may take your good friend to bed. Come back now and we'll forget all about a traditional wedding night.* That particular idea had been one of the stupidest plans he'd ever come up with.

When he'd finally let Jill Ellis into Meg's office, before he'd lost his mind completely and made love to Emma, Jill had looked very suspiciously at the pair of them. Emma had covered for them by claiming they'd been having a disagreement over the wedding and that's why they hadn't heard her knock. She had then fled. He thought he'd handled it well until Jill had left and he'd run to the men's bathroom to look at himself in the mirror. Then he'd seen what Jill had been staring at—lipstick on one corner of his mouth.

Over the phone to the woman he loved he said, "I miss you."

"I miss you too, but the book..."

For once he wished he was more important than any damn book. He needed Meg back in town soon. He needed to see her, to touch her. To know that he loved her. To prove that he loved her. If Meg would only come back today, he'd make love to her until she never wanted to leave him again.

"If you came back now, we could elope," he offered half-heartedly.

"Darling!" Meg said, sounding shocked. "After all the preparations for the wedding? We can't do that. I wouldn't want to betray Emma like that. You know she's had a bad experience with weddings. Besides, Zoe Dixon isn't going to make the deadline unless I'm with her, coaching her through the end of the story." She paused a minute and then hurried on, as if offering a confession. "It's rather exciting out here. All the swimming pools and narcissism. Everyone is blatant in their ambition and in their search for physical perfection. It's kind of weird, but I like it. I saw Rosie O'Donnell having lunch with Nicole Kidman yesterday. It's so different from New York. Kind of like an...adventure. I think I've gotten so used to the way people behave in my little world, in publishing, that I've forgotten there are other possibilities."

Something struck him about the way she said the word *adventure*, but he didn't understand what. "Rosie who?"

"Rosie O'Donnell. She's the new queen of daytime TV."

"I didn't know you watched TV talk shows."

"I guess there's a lot of things the two of us don't know about each other."

She sounded a little worried and he hastened to reassure her. "We'll have a lifetime to find out. After the wedding."

"After the wedding. Of course, you're right. Darling..." She paused rather deliberately. "It'll only be for a few more days, I promise. Being away from Scorpion and you and the family and everything, well, it's just giving me a lot of time to think...."

"Is something wrong, Meg?"

"No, nothing's wrong. I was only thinking that I've been so busy I've just fallen into a lot of assumptions about what I should do."

"Meg?" He waited. Was she having second thoughts about them, as well? Reconsidering...?

"And I realized that marrying you is the smartest thing I could do with my life," Meg said firmly. Why didn't he feel happier at her words? Meg lowered her voice and he responded to its smoky promise. "I'm so sorry about the delay. But I'll make it up to you once I'm back. Our wedding night is only eight nights away."

He closed his eyes. "I know. But it would be better if you came back soon."

Worry entered her voice. "Is something else wrong? More trouble with Scorpion? Jay?" She said her brother's name with fear.

"No, nothing new." Max didn't mention the announcement that Peter Cooper was about to make in just a few minutes. He'd tried to talk Peter out of it, but since the news about Scorpion was going to be in the newspapers tomorrow anyway, there was little either of them could do. "I just miss you."

"Darling, you're going to have a lifetime of me. A few days now won't make any difference."

A few more days with a she-devil temptress just might. "The wedding…" He tried again. "I could use your advice. I'm really out of my depth with all the…the stuff."

"I trust you and Emma implicitly. You and Emma. I trust you both."

EMMA WAVED AT Amy Severn and made her way to where the art department was gathered in the lobby, waiting for Peter Cooper's announcement.

"I bet he's inviting us all to a special party for Mr. Thorne and Miss Cooper," Adele Milkens whispered. She pushed her straight, black-as-the-dead-of-night hair out of her eyes and surveyed the entire staff of Scorpion Books, which was assembled in the lobby, through her kohl-outlined eyes. "I hope the party is in the city and not at their estate. Nature makes me nervous."

Emma hoped Peter Cooper was inviting everyone to a party, but she feared not. She'd had little time to concern herself with Scorpion, having spent the better part of five days in and out of the building attending to the wedding, talking to the aunts from Atlanta and liaising with Beth. Emma and Sarah Tepper had even managed a fitting for their bridesmaid dresses.

Back in Philadelphia Susan was booking appointments with brides; she wasn't committing Emma to anything until Emma had a chance to speak to each and every bride personally. She always wanted to know if their personalities meshed. And from now on she'd insist upon meeting the groom well ahead of the ceremony!

Her business was so small in comparision to the Coopers' company. Emma hadn't realized how many employees Scorpion had on its payroll. Moreover, the head office was only part of the operation. There was a small editorial office in Los Angeles, with strong connections to the movie business. Then there was the printing plant and distribution center in New Jersey. She agreed with Max that whoever was stealing from Scorpion had to be working out of head office. Someone she had met. Someone standing with her in the lobby, feigning innocence.

Peter Cooper had worked hard, had put much of his soul into Scorpion Books. He had bought the company, originally a vanity press that printed customers' books for a fee, and had retained the design and production staff. At first he had been the only editor and had even had to advertise for manuscripts. Out of the slush pile—as she'd learned the huge pile of manuscripts from unpublished writers was called—Peter had culled his first gems. *The Regular Guy's Guide to Investing* had been Scorpion Books's first minor success. It had been followed by a book on dog grooming and then several action-adventure books that had developed a cult following.

At that time, Scorpion had used only the twelfth floor of

the building and Peter had rented out the other floors. Today, they controlled the entire building. Other than the editorial department, which included the acquisition and development editors and the copy editors, there were more divisions than a nonbook person like herself could have imagined: art, marketing, publicity, promotion, finance and management information systems, otherwise known as the computer geeks. Over a hundred and fifty full-time employees filled Scorpion's hallways throughout the days and nights. No matter how late Emma left the building, she always left a dedicated few behind. She wondered how Max could ever decide who to investigate; he did seem to be a one-man operation. While she had chatted up the art staff—all obvious suspects—the real thief could be in the mail room. Her amateur investigation hadn't revealed anything other than the fact that many employees didn't like their immediate superior. Not exactly an earthshattering revelation. She sighed. This was becoming way too complicated. Including her feelings for Max.

The crowd moved slightly, allowing Peter Cooper to take the center. He looked around, realized that not everyone would be able to see him, and jumped on top of the security guard's desk. Emma laughed with the rest at the CEO's easy athleticism and lack of concern about maintaining the proper dignity.

"Friends…" He raised his hands to quiet the group.

"Where are the drinks?" Art Spiegle, the head of production, shouted from the back. "How can we toast our success without champagne?" Such a roar of approval followed that Emma clapped as well. This morning she had learned that advance word from the *New York Times* included two Scorpion books on the list. She knew that making the *New York Times* list was the pinnacle for every publisher and author. Once an author had NYT, he or she had the designation forever. It was rumored that many such authors had requested

New York Times Bestselling Author be engraved on their tombstone.

"I agree we have much to celebrate, thanks to your hard work, and to the upcoming nuptials of my daughter and Scorpion's newest vice president. But that, unfortunately, is not why I've assembled us together. I'm afraid I have some very bad news, which I have been keeping to myself. But the story is going to be in tomorrow's paper and I'd rather you heard it from me than read it at your breakfast table."

There was silence and uneasy shuffling. "What is he talking about?" Adele Milken asked. "I'm getting a nervous feeling about this."

"My friends," Peter Cooper repeated. "I'm not sure how to say this, so...the truth is..." He looked around and saw Emma. She gave him an encouraging smile, but he still seemed lost.

Max walked over to Peter and jumped onto the desk next to him. "Scorpion Books is in bad financial trouble. Someone has been duplicating our cover film, then printing covers and returning them."

"How could that be?" Art Spiegle cried.

"This is awful!" a young woman's voice declared.

Those were the last sentences Emma was able to distinguish as the crowd broke into a furious babble. Peter raised his hands, silencing them. He had their full attention now. "I wanted you to know the difficulties we're facing, but we're not beaten. I'm going to figure out how this is happening and stop it. But in the meantime, our security measures are being changed. Once cover film has been approved by editorial, art and marketing, it will be delivered to me. I'll be the one looking after it until we find out who is behind this sabotage." His voice broke on the last word and Emma felt her heart go out to him. She watched as Peter Cooper surveyed his employees. Someone in the crowd was determined to hurt him and perhaps ruin Scorpion Books, his lifetime achievement.

BETRAYAL. Maxwell Frasier Thorne wondered what Meg would think of him when he told her the truth. What she would say to him. Would she tell him she loved him or would she be glad for the excuse to cancel their wedding?

He was a different man now, he reminded himself. As soon as Meg returned from Los Angeles he would tell her everything about his past with Emma. What he needed to concentrate on at the moment was his investigation and keeping away from the bridal consultant.

Unfortunately, the evidence was pointing to Jay as the guilty party. His signature was on the early thefts, the only covers they knew for sure had been double run. On more recent titles, Jay was being less blatant. Then there was his free-spending life-style. His inability to restrain his passions. Max recognized the weaknesses in Jay.

Suddenly the woman who threatened everything he'd worked for burst into his office. "It's Brenda Lau," Emma exclaimed.

"It's late," he said, trying to ignore how her excitement flushed her cheeks and made her eyes sparkle. He put the background folders on Jay and his other suspects into his desk drawer and locked it. There was nothing incriminating in any of the dockets other than Jay's: no sudden large bank deposits, no big purchases and nothing to provide any kind of motive. While the crime could be simple theft, he guessed there was another motive. Jay had a lot of reasons to be angry at his father.

"Of course it's late. I've been investigating. What are you doing?"

"I'm trying to finish the second quarters' reports."

"But it's Brenda," she repeated.

Sighing, he took off his glasses. "What about Brenda?"

"She's the one. The guilty party. Stealing money from Scorpion."

"Don't be ridiculous. She's a brilliant controller."

"So who knows better how to steal? I was on my way home but I got sidetracked in the lobby—" He could imagine. Emma spent every day gossiping with everyone in the company. How she actually managed to pull a wedding together he didn't know. "Then I remembered I'd left the list of songs in Meg's office, so I went back. When I got close, I saw the door was partially open—I'd locked it—and when I peered in I saw Brenda Lau."

He was taken aback. What would Brenda Lau, corporate controller, be doing in Meg's office, especially since Emma had taken over its use? Brenda? That seemed too unlikely. She was hardworking and ambitious and determined—much like himself when he'd been at McCord Industries. Instead he said, "Corporate investigations involve a lot more than sneaking around corridors and riffling through desks, Emma."

"I want to help you and that's all I know how to do. Please, Max. Don't you think it's weird?" When Emma turned soft and pleading like this, he had a hard time resisting.

"Yes," he agreed, and stood up. "Why don't we have a talk with Brenda?" Anything so that he wouldn't be alone with Emma.

"This is so great." Emma practically skipped down the hallway.

"That Brenda is guilty?"

"Yes. No. Oh, you know what I mean. That Jay isn't the one. Peter Cooper looked so sad today when he told everyone about what was going on."

"Do you think it will make him any happier that one of his trusted employees is the guilty one?" Over the years Max had learned that in a situation like this one there was no real happy ending.

"You're twisting my words and my meaning. All of this is awful, Max, but there's nothing worse than being betrayed by someone you love."

He didn't say anything but knew it was true. He'd betrayed Emma once; he wasn't about to do the same to Meg. No matter what kinds of feelings were being awakened in him. Besides, his feelings were only lust.

Max stopped outside Brenda's office, which was dark but Emma sensed movement inside. "Why would Brenda be hiding in the dark in her office, unless she has something to hide?" she whispered.

"Exactly," he said, and she knew he was referring to their kiss. She felt her face grow hot with shame. She'd already apologized to him for her behavior.

She still couldn't believe that she'd dared him to kiss her. Max never backed down from a challenge.

Thank goodness Jill Ellis had come to Meg's office to return a manuscript and stopped them from going any farther. Emma had been so lost that she wasn't sure if she would have stopped Max if he'd...if he'd made love to her.

There, she'd thought it.

She, Emma Grace Delany—conniving bridal consultant; duplicitous, back-stabbing friend—had wanted Maxwell Frasier Thorne to make love to her. To prove to herself that he wanted her more than he wanted Meg. To prove that he'd no more forgotten her than she'd forgotten him.

Well, she'd proven to herself what a bad friend she could be, and she wasn't going to tempt Max again. After all, she needed to remember that he was a man. A man who hadn't had sex recently. His reaction to her had been due to hormones, not lingering feelings. She'd taught herself a hard lesson.

Max knocked softly on Brenda's door. "Just a minute," Brenda called out, and they heard a desk drawer slam shut. "Come in," she called again, brightly this time, as if she wasn't hiding in the dark.

They entered the controller's small office, lit only by a desk light. "Frasier, Emma?" Brenda said in surprise. "I didn't expect anyone else to be here so late tonight." Her voice had a funny quaver to it.

Max fixed Brenda with the "confess now" look that Emma usually experienced from him. "I'm finishing up the second-quarter reports and learning that a bridal consultant's work is never done," he said. "Why were you in Meg's office earlier this evening?" His voice became so steely he scared Emma.

Brenda flinched, but raised her chin. "I don't know what you're talking about. I wasn't..." she stopped and turned to Emma. "You."

"I saw you," Emma said simply.

Brenda shook her head. "I waited for you to go home. But when I was in Meg's office, I thought I heard someone in the corridor. Just my luck to get caught in my one little dishonest act."

Now Emma was beginning to hope that Brenda had some reasonable explanation for sneaking into Meg's office. "I was talking to Adele in the lobby and then realized I'd forgotten some paperwork. So I went back upstairs." She sighed. "Why were you in Meg's office?"

Brenda bit her lip and her shoulders slumped. "I was never any good at lying. I...this is so embarrassing but, well, I've always wanted to be an editor." When Emma and Max stared at her blankly, she shrugged her shoulders, opening her arms wide, hands palm up. "Look at me. I'm Chinese. I'm supposed to be good at numbers."

"You are," said Max.

"Yes, and my family expected me to choose a respectable profession."

"Editing isn't respectable?" asked Emma.

"Not really. At least not according to my family. The pay is lousy, you can get fired whenever there's a change at the top and nobody ever really understands what you do."

Emma had never thought of it that way.

"My family wasn't very happy when I took this finance job with Scorpion Books, because I make so much less than I would on Wall Street, but we all agreed it was an acceptable compromise. Only it isn't enough for me. I'm surrounded by books, but all I get to work on are the numbers."

Brenda looked at Max pleadingly. "You have to believe me. I would never do anything to hurt Scorpion Books. This is where I've always wanted to be. Plus Meg is so nice. I talked to her about books and my ideas, and after I'd bent her ear for over a year she finally asked me why I was in corporate finance. She offered to help train me with line editing. She said I had a lot of the other skills, but needed hands-on experience with manuscripts. We spoke today and Meg told me there was a manuscript in her office that I could start editing." Brenda opened her desk drawer and pulled out a pile of papers. From the title page Emma read *Dieting Can be Deadly*.

"Nonfiction?"

"No, murder at a health spa." Brenda sparkled as she began to talk about the book. "The heroine is a talk show host, sort of like Oprah, who has slipped on her exercise regime recently and then goes to a health spa where the owner is murdered. The talk show host investigates. I've worked with the author on revisions and Meg thought I could handle the line edit. Eve Dean, the head of publicity, thinks she might be able to get the author on *Oprah!*" Brenda breathed the last words in a rush of excitement.

"But why didn't you simply ask Emma if you could look through Meg's office for the manuscript?" Max asked, clearly puzzled.

"Because I'm not sure if I'll be a good editor. I've been keeping my desire a secret until I know I can do it. Then I have to tell my parents first, so that they can prepare themselves. They'll never understand." Brenda shook her head sadly. "If I become an editor, they're going to be very disappointed with me."

Ouch, Emma thought. Brenda's explanation was so off-the-wall that it had to be true. "We're sorry to have disturbed you," Emma said as she pulled Max toward the door. Max was right. She wasn't any good at this investigation stuff.

Max lead her away from Brenda's office, around the corner to the editorial department, and began the lecture that she was expecting. "Investigating is a lot more than following suspects around. Motive, opportunity, past history are more... What was that?"

Emma, too, had heard the sound and turned to run toward the noise. But he stopped her.

She looked around. "Here," she whispered, and pulled open a supply cupboard, tugging him in after her. It was a tight fit, but they managed. Max kept the door open, and the muted, nighttime lights showed a figure unlocking Sarah Tepper's office door.

"Who is it?" Emma whispered into his ear.

"Be quiet," he ordered, waiting for the figure to reappear. After a few minutes, the figure came out of Sarah's office carrying something.

"He has something in his hands. We have to stop him!"

Max held Emma still. "No, we don't. I recognized him."

"Who was it?" she demanded, and then she saw his face. "Oh no."

"It was Jay."

The family of the bride invites you...

8

"I CAN'T BELIEVE Jay has done anything wrong," Peter Cooper said as he unlocked the door to Sarah Tepper's office. After Max telephoned him, Peter had rushed back to the office. "He was probably looking for Sarah, or maybe even leaving a present for her. You've seen how infatuated he is with the young woman. Best choice he's made in years."

Peter flicked on the lights and Emma saw lines of worry etched on his face. He might claim to believe in his son, but his expression showed another truth. The fact that he'd hired a private investigator like Max rather than going to the police also revealed that he was afraid. What would Peter Cooper do if his son was guilty? Would he hand him over to the authorities?

"You must be right," Emma agreed, despite her misgivings. She was tired of her thoughts, which just went round and round. This tension about the identity of the thief was eating away at her, so it had to be doubly bad for Peter. "He probably left a gift for Sarah to find in the morning. It was silly of him not to realize that sneaking around into other people's offices was a bad idea—"

Peter made a strangled sound and then collapsed onto one of the white leather chairs.

"What?" she asked, not really wanting to hear the answer. She felt sick.

Peter covered his face with his hands and moaned. He actually moaned. There was no brightly wrapped package on Sarah's desk, but there was a brown envelope. Emma stared at it with dread as Peter said, "The cover film. I hid the mechanicals in Sarah's office."

Max handed Peter the envelope and he opened it slowly. Emma wanted to scream at him to hurry up and tell them, but when he raised defeated eyes to them, she didn't need to hear his words. "Two of the final proofs are missing. There were eight, now there are only six. Somebody has stolen them."

"No," Emma said weakly. It couldn't be Jay. It would destroy Peter and Meg.

Max stood very still in the center of the room. "What do you want me to do now?"

"Investigate some more, dammit! The evidence may be piling up against my son, but he is not guilty. There has to be another explanation."

Max studied the wounded man and then nodded his head. "I've hired an outside firm to do background checks on the key players. I'll have them widen their field, but I'm also going to have Jay followed."

A miserable Peter Cooper nodded briefly, then closed his eyes. "He's my son. He can't be trying to ruin us." Through sheer force of will, Peter pulled himself together slowly, a much older man now than when he'd entered Sarah's office. He walked to the door and then turned around. "Find out the truth."

Emma and Max stood frozen for a minute, staring at each other. She wished she could throw herself into his arms and he'd promise that everything was going to be okay. *Bad idea, Emma*, she told herself and bolted from the office, following Peter Cooper to the elevator. She heard Max behind her.

Peter stood by the elevator, not raising his head when they joined him. Max pushed the button, which the elder Cooper hadn't touched, and the doors opened almost immediately.

"I'll find out the truth," Max promised as he stepped inside with Peter and Meg.

"I know you will. I'm glad my daughter had the good sense to fall in love with you, Frasier Thorne. She'll always be able to rely on you."

"Yes. Yes, she will."

"It's all going to turn out okay," Emma reassured Peter.

"My daughter's lucky to have a good friend like you." The senior Cooper squeezed her hand. The elevator pinged and the doors opened to the lobby. Peter stepped out first, practically knocking over Mrs. Daley, who was exiting from the other elevator. As always, she was dressed immaculately in a navy blue suit, carrying a briefcase and her trench coat.

"Excuse me," she said, panting slightly. "I ran for the elevator."

"Here, let me help you with your coat," Peter gallantly offered his assistant.

She looked somewhat taken aback, then handed over her coat. "You're working very late tonight, Mr. Cooper."

"Good heavens, woman, no one seems to work more than you. I don't know what Scorpion Books or I would do without you."

"Oh you." She blushed.

"Seriously!" Peter twinkled at her. "You know you're the woman of my dreams." He kissed her lightly on her cheek. "Let me take your briefcase."

"No need..." She held on for a moment, but then gave in when it became clear Peter wasn't about to accept no for an answer. "Thank you. You are always such a gentleman. I tell my son Arnold that all the time. That he should learn to be as polite a gentleman as Mr. Cooper."

"I hope Arnold is doing well since he came back home."

"Yes. The new job you helped him get suits him. He likes being a security guard. It gives him a lot of time to read."

"Excellent. I'll drive you home. I'm heading back to Long Island tonight."

The older pair left, and Emma thought once again about Peter Cooper's words. That he wanted Max to find out the truth. "Ouch." Emma spoke her thoughts out loud to Max. "I think I like my job a lot better than yours. I deal with hysterical mothers and anxious brides, but my biggest life-and-death decisions are crepe de chine or satin. How can you do this?"

"For justice. It's worth the price to do the right thing."

"But if Jay is the one betraying Scorpion Books it might kill Peter Cooper."

"The old man is strong—he'll get past it even if Jay is the guilty one. But we haven't closed our case yet. Remember innocent until proven guilty."

"Do you think he's innocent?" she couldn't help asking.

"No. Come on, I'll drive you home."

"You can walk me. I'm staying at Meg's apartment. You know the way, of course." Wanting to lighten their mood, to return them to their easier sparring days, she said, "Although I guess you don't know the way to her bedroom, right?"

"You're pushing me too far," he growled as he grabbed her arm and pulled her close to him.

"Yes?" she asked, her senses alert.

Instead of replying he pushed her away from him. "I'll walk with you. This city is dangerous at night."

Not nearly as dangerous as Maxwell Frasier Thorne was to her self-control.

EMMA HIT THE ALARM CLOCK hard, wishing she could kick her conscience just as hard. Her head felt like she was suffering from a terrible hangover. She realized she was, remembering that she had tried to drown her sorrows last night. "Stupid plan," she muttered, and dragged herself out of bed.

What had she been thinking of? She took two aspirins with a glass of water, knowing exactly what she'd been thinking of. Max.

She continued to call herself an idiot in the bathroom mirror until the phone rang. Meg had a portable model, and last night Emma had called some old friends. Now she couldn't remember where she'd left it. Finally unearthing it from a basket of embroidery, she said hello.

"Emma dear, is that you? I trust I didn't interrupt at an inopportune moment. You sound out of breath," Daisy Winslow said.

"Oh no, I just lost the phone." Emma let the silence hang; she wasn't going to explain.

"Of course, dear. I called because we finished designing the centerpieces, which are all splendid and very pink, and the place cards. Beth had the brilliant idea of stenciling Frasier and Meg's names onto the napkins inside a heart, and that took over two days, but now we're through with our tasks. We thought perhaps that we would take the day off and do some shopping in the city. My sister and I wanted to buy something very special for our Meg and her fiancé."

The aunts in New York. Emma wondered if the city could survive the pair's critical assessment. "That's a wonderful idea. I've had you working much too hard. In fact, if you can spare the time I'd like to take you out to lunch."

"That would be very lovely."

"Come by the Scorpion offices," Emma said, knowing the sisters wanted to see the famed publishing company but wouldn't ask for an invitation, "then we'll choose a restaurant."

Daisy agreed upon the time and hung up. "This should be interesting," Emma announced to the empty room. No matter what people thought of her career, it was never dull.

ONE WEEK, Maxwell Frasier Thorne told himself. One week until the wedding. *Hold on.* Only days until his fiancée returned to him and his lonely bed. He'd sweep her off her feet and make love to her like a man possessed.

Because he was possessed.

But not by Megan Elizabeth Cooper.

"One week," he muttered as he heard a babble of female voices. He restrained himself from hiding underneath his desk. The last time he'd heard a group of females outside his office, he'd been dragged off to the art department, to an impromptu workshop where he'd been forced to help wrap vases in fabric. He still didn't really understand why; it had something to do with the flowers for the tables at the wedding, but he didn't see what necessitated sticking a piece of pleated fabric around a vase. He'd tried to say so, but had been silenced so quickly that he'd completed his work and escaped at the first opportunity.

The details of the wedding didn't matter to him. What mattered was that he'd been happy with Meg in the past and he'd be happy with her again. Under no circumstances was he about to betray her. He was no longer the Max Thorne who lied, who stole, who disappeared in the middle of the night.

He'd learned to tame his appetites. Emma was a tempting hors d'oeuvre but he wasn't about to sample.

The woman who was the cause of all his troubles and conflicts walked into his office, leading the aunts from Atlanta. "Oh my." Primrose fluttered her hands as she looked around the elegantly furnished executive office. Max had never given much thought to his office. He'd left everything as he'd found it, as he'd known his job was only temporary. Primrose caressed one of his leather chairs. "I never realized before how *masculine* you are, my dear Mr. Thorne."

"Frasier, you must call me Frasier." He was on his feet ushering the two women to chairs, offering coffee, bottled water.

"No, nothing for us now," Daisy declared. "Our delightful new friend Emma, such a sweet girl, is taking us out for lunch. The Russian Tea Room," she declared. "Why, I've read all about it in that *People* mag—"

"Never mind all that gossip," Primrose interrupted, clearly not as impressed by a fancy Manhattan eatery. "We wanted to discuss a very serious issue." He raised his head in surprise, wondering if Primrose suspected something. "We want to give you and Meg a wedding gift you'll always remember."

"Meg and I are thrilled that you were able to come for the wedding. Your help with the wedding preparations while Meg's been out of town has been invaluable. We couldn't ask for more."

"Yes, well, I must admit it is odd for the bride to disappear so close to the wedding date, but young people these days are so different from our generation." Primrose sniffed. "When is Meg coming back?"

"Tomorrow, I hope." Today would be even better. Emma was dressed in a short green skirt and Max was having a hard time keeping his gaze away from her legs. He ached to run his hands along her firm calves, maybe tickle her behind her knees and then explore farther up her soft thighs.... "What?" he asked.

"I was saying only a week to the wedding." Daisy sighed. "I remember the first wedding I ever attended. It was at Christmas and everything was white."

"I suggested the ladies might give you some kind of a family heirloom, perhaps a tea service," Emma said.

"We agreed that a family heirloom might be just the thing, as Meg has so little from her mother's side, but a tea service seems so terribly impractical for young people. You're all rush, rush, rush, take-out food and breakfast meetings. A leisurely visit and tea is only a fond memory of the past, so..." Primrose trailed off, building anticipation.

"We thought we'd give you the Blue House," Daisy added excitedly.

"The Blue House." Was this some kind of china pattern? Or maybe one of those collectable things that some women kept? Dolls or porcelain houses and other peculiar items. He realized that neither Meg nor Emma collected things. So far it was the only trait they had in common. Other than agreeing to marry him.

"The Blue House," Emma repeated. "It's a house. In Charleston."

"Yes, the family hasn't used it for years, and we've been considering renting it out, but it just never felt right," Primrose said. "Then Daisy wished she could see more of you and Meg once you were married, so a home in Charleston seems just the answer. It's not very big, only six bedrooms, but we thought it might serve you as a vacation getaway. Maybe Meg could bring some of her author friends and have a writer's retreat at the house. Wouldn't that be fun," she suggested, clearly more a fan of literature than celebrity spotting.

He sat back in his chair, completely flummoxed. A house. The sweet little old ladies wanted to give them a house as a wedding present so he and Meg would have some place to stay in Charleston! The life-style he was marrying into hit him hard. He'd always known Meg's family was well-to-do, but he'd tried not to let it worry him. The old money from Meg's mother's side, however, was overwhelming. He didn't care about the money but he did care about being accepted into the family and returning their trust.

Or was he marrying into one of the families he'd always been envious of?

"Ladies, I don't know what to say. Your offer is very generous and I would love to see your fine city of Charleston and visit with you, but I must confer with Meg before we can accept." He hoped Meg would be able to think of some gracious way for them to decline the gift. A house in Charleston seemed so final. So married.

He started. Why did he shiver at the thought of marriage? It was what he wanted.

"We understand completely. It's nice how husbands and wives consult each other these days. That is a pleasant change." Primrose stood. "Come, Daisy."

Max opened the door for them, and walked straight into the fight.

"I CAN'T BELIEVE my own father thinks I'm a criminal!" Jay yelled, his face red with fury.

Peter Cooper held up his arms to appease his son. "I don't. I want to believe you're innocent."

"Want to believe. That means you don't believe!"

"Son, I do trust you."

"Ha!" Jay stormed past him into his father's office. He came back out and noticed the crowd gathered in the hallway, attracted by the shouting. He pointed at Max and Emma. "You two, in here. The rest of you—don't you have work to do?"

Emma and Max, followed by Daisy and Primrose, walked into Peter's office. Max shut the door firmly. If only she and the aunts could have escaped five minutes ago, they would have missed this scene. They could be dining in fine style and gossiping over celebrities instead of having to experience this family unpleasantness.

"We're family now," Primrose said firmly. "We're staying to find out what's going on."

"You two were spying on me last night," Jay accused Emma and Max.

"No, they weren't." Mr. Cooper hurried to clarify. "But I have asked everyone to report any suspicious activity to me. Frasier and Emma did as I asked."

"And what were the two of them doing together so late here at the office?"

"We have a wedding to plan," Max said calmly.

"I hope it's your wedding to my sister that you're planning. With the amount of time you two spend together, and the looks you give each other, I'm beginning to wonder if my sister will have a wedding to return to."

"Jay, you're upset. Frasier and your sister are in love."

Jay turned on his father again. "Why aren't you suspicious of this pair? They were here late at night. They could be planting evidence against me. I am your son. You should trust me."

"I do." Peter sighed. "The problem is that you sneaked into Sarah's office. I put the cover film there. Two pieces are missing."

Jay turned pale. "Surely you don't suspect Sarah...."

"No. Sarah was giving a lecture at NYU last night. And you were the one seen entering her office. What were you doing there?"

"Nothing," he answered.

"But I saw you," Emma protested. "And it looked like you had something in your hands when you left her office."

"You couldn't have seen what—if anything—I was holding. It was dark."

"No, I couldn't," she was forced to admit.

"Then you have no proof. And I wasn't stealing the cover film. I would never hurt Scorpion Books." He looked at the group, his face earnest, but Emma had to wonder. Why wouldn't he tell them what he'd been doing in Sarah's office?

"You're all going to have to take my word for it that I'm not the thief."

It was fine for Jay to make that demand, but he couldn't be aware of how he was hurting all those who cared the most about him. Including Sarah. When Emma and Sarah had spoken this morning over coffee, Sarah had admitted she had no idea what Jay had been doing in her office. She'd shaken her head with worry, saying, "What have I done to him?"

"You should believe Jay," Daisy suddenly announced.

"Of course I trust my own son," Peter Cooper said, sinking into his executive chair as if his body was too weary to hold him upright any longer. "But I just don't know what to do anymore."

"If you need money, we could lend it to you," Primrose offered.

"That's very sweet of you, but I need quite a bit of money." Peter named what to Emma was an astronomical amount.

"Well," Primrose said with a gasp. "That's a healthy figure, but Daisy and I can manage it. I'll have my banker make the proper arrangements. But the question you have to ask yourself is who wants to hurt you? If Scorpion Books suffers, then you suffer."

"Of course," Max said suddenly. He smiled at Primrose and kissed her on the cheek.

"Oh, my!" she said, pink and flustered.

Max smiled again, then turned to Peter Cooper. "That's exactly the key that's been missing! I have to go." He threw open the door, knocking aside Mrs. Daley, who'd been hovering outside.

Taking her elbows, Max moved Mrs. Daley out of the way. "Excuse me," he said, and ran down the hallway.

"My, he has a lot of energy," Primrose commented admiringly. "Meg is one lucky girl."

Yes, Emma agreed silently. Only she worried that Meg had no idea how lucky she was and didn't appreciate Max nearly enough. On Meg's return, Emma vowed to have a good talk with her, convince her how wonderful Max was. How she shouldn't make him second in her priorities.

At the moment she said, "Lunch," as brightly as she could manage, and the two ladies nodded.

"The Russian Tea Room," Daisy enthused once again. "Do you think Dustin Hoffmann might be there? He's such an attractive young man. Or that Warren Beatty. I'm so glad he finally married. I was worried he'd grow old and still behave like a silly young boy."

"I'm sure we'll see someone famous," Emma assured them as she steered the two women toward the elevator. After this fiasco, however, she'd need Tom Cruise, George Clooney and Harrison Ford, all lunching together at the very next table, to appease her own spirits.

Everything was going from bad to worse.

At this rate, the band would forget to show, the caterer would give everyone food poisoning and the bridesmaids would have to walk down the aisle in track suits. No matter what, she was going to make sure that Meg and Max made it to the preacher.

They were going to be happy even if it killed her!

One last fling...

"MAX." Emma whispered his name as he walked away from the photocopier. "Max." Her voice was louder now.

He stopped and wondered what he had ever done to deserve this. Oh, he knew what he'd done—and what he wanted to do. But he was trying his best to do what he was supposed to. Find out who was stealing money from Scorpion Books. Marry Meg.

He *was* marrying Meg. Whenever he looked at Emma and thought about... Well, whenever he looked at Emma, he needed to remember he was about to enter into holy wedlock with Meg. They were going to spend the rest of their lives together. Have a family. She was his future. She would let him be the kind of man he wanted to be. Meg was the perfect woman for him.

"Over here," Emma's voice announced. He looked around but didn't see anyone in the cubbyhole area. A gray metal shelf filled with paper for the photocopier stood next to a large wooden table covered with courier packages waiting for pickup. Empty boxes filled the space beneath the table. There was no Emma in sight, but she was here somewhere. Investigating. No matter what he said, she would go ahead and do whatever she decided was the right thing to do. And since friends were involved, she'd be even more determined. The hopeless romantic also believed that things would work out for the best. That a happy ending was possible. Silly fool.

Hadn't he already proved to her that happy endings didn't always happen?

"Where?" he asked the empty space, feeling ridiculous. Emma always made him feel inappropriate emotions. If he'd stayed with her, he would have ruined both of them.

"Here."

He willed himself to speak calmly and slowly. "I'm going to look very strange talking to myself if anyone walks by. Everyone's staying as far away from me as possible already."

"Oh." Some boxes under the table shifted and part of Emma's ankle appeared. He shouldn't be able to recognize her ankle after eight years, but he did. He moved aside one of the bigger boxes, grabbed her arm and helped her climb out from under the table.

"Hiding from the aunts?"

"Oh, no. They're absolute dears." Emma brushed dust off her short brown sweater and then her black fitted trousers. He tore his eyes away from her narrow waist and gently flared hips. "Daisy almost passed out when we saw Woody Allen. Even Primrose was impressed, but I think that's because she considers him a writer."

"I did rather notice that Primrose has a strong interest in publishing, Scorpion Books in particular. I almost expect her to show up here any day now with a large manuscript under her arm—a story she's been working on for the last twenty years or so. Like that old lady in the nursing home who wrote that bestseller."

"*Ladies of the Club.* You certainly have immersed yourself in publishing stories."

"Part of the job."

"And part of your new family."

"Yes." Meg's family. Soon to be his, he reminded himself yet again.

"Primrose was very quick to offer the money to Peter,"

Emma continued. "It was as if it was her opportunity to become part of the publishing company. You don't think she and Daisy could have planned...?"

"No," he said firmly. "I think Primrose seized an opportunity. One Peter Cooper may have to take her up on." When he and Peter had spoken this afternoon the old man had looked very worried. And there was little Max had been able to say to reassure him. "We got more bad coverage in the papers today and our printers are demanding we pay for their work before they go to press."

"That's outrageous."

"Yes," Max had agreed tiredly. He wished he had another suspect to give Peter Cooper other than Jay, but he didn't. There had been a brief period when he'd wondered if the elder Cooper was sabotaging his own company for the publicity. Scorpion was taking up a lot of space in the entertainment section of the papers these days, where their lead titles were listed along with every story. From what little Max knew about publishing people, they were willing to do almost anything to sell books. He'd even considered Eve Dean, the head of publicity, but the losses were too significant for that. No, Jay was looking more and more guilty. Still, for Meg and her father, Max would keep looking. Maybe, with luck, he could find another suspect.

His job had become more difficult, however, as everyone at Scorpion was now wary of him. A number of people had looked at him suspiciously, but that was only to be expected. He was the outsider who had successfully become part of the Cooper family in a very short period of time. He was about to marry the woman who would run the company one day. No one except Emma and Mr. Cooper knew his real role at Scorpion Books. Until now he'd been able to run the background checks, study all the financial records and spend a lot of time in the office without raising any questions. That was no longer possible.

"What in the world were you doing?"

"Oh, Max, you'll never believe what just happened." He waited, knowing it was impossible to stop Emma once she got going. "I saw Art Spiegle—I remembered what you said about having a funny feeling about him. Anyway, he was with a group of really tough-looking men. I tried to get close enough to hear them when they disappeared into the lunchroom, but then when they hurried out, I had to hide."

"Meg, corporate investigation is more than hiding in hallways," he began, and then heard voices.

"It's them," Emma exclaimed, and pulled him into the nearby cupboard. As he pressed himself into the small space next to Emma, he was forced to reconsider his position. Perhaps corporate investigation *was* hiding in hallways. Certainly Emma had more suspects than he did.

They stood only inches apart, and Max suddenly remembered the time Emma had dragged him into a supply cupboard and they had made wild, passionate love. He heard her quick intake of breath. Their eyes met, and from the flare of heat, he saw that she was remembering as well.

Unable to help himself, he touched her cheek. Soft color flooded her skin. He traced his fingers over her lips and they opened under the gentle pressure. He leaned even closer to her and her gaze fixed on his mouth, only a breath away from hers.

He needed to pull himself back from the madness. "I recognize Art's voice," he said coolly. Anger flared across Emma's face and she tried to push herself away from him, but he refused to budge. He pressed even closer to her, wanting to make her suffer as much as he was. To make her suffer as much as he did every day she was around. "Quiet," he whispered.

From their vantage point they could view the elevators as Art Speigle and the three tough-looking men walked to it. Art pushed the Down button. The normally unflappable head of production shook as he said goodbye to his visitors. His round face was shining; Max could see a gleam of sweat on the man's upper lip.

Art couldn't be nearly as unsettled as Max was, pressed against Emma. Her curves fit against him so well. Unable to resist, since he was already in agony, he slid one hand down Emma's back, curving it around her behind, pulling her even tighter against him.

"Stop that," she whispered into his ear, but her words sounded more like a plea to continue. She wrapped her arms around his neck.

He buried his groan against her throat and then raised his head to see the tallest Asian man say, "We're agreed then." The man touched the breast of his tailored jacket.

"Yes," Art said quickly, his eyes fixed on the man's jacket. *A gun?* Max wondered.

"Good," said a much younger, ponytailed man. The elevator pinged and the doors opened. He slapped Art on the shoulder. Art flinched and then let himself be led onto the elevator.

Max and Emma were left alone, wrapped in each other's arms. Very slowly, he moved his hand back up her body, along the flare of her waist, brushing the side of her breast until he cupped her face and lowered his mouth—

Emma broke free of his embrace. She fluffed her hair nervously and wouldn't meet his eyes. "Don't tell me that wasn't strange. Before, when I was hiding behind the boxes, I heard them threaten Artie." She shivered. "They called him that—*Artie.*"

If Emma wanted to pretend that nothing had happened between them, Max was willing to go along with her. He had to remember that nothing was *going* to happen between them.

What she had told him was odd, Max was forced to agree. But it didn't mean he wanted Emma conducting any more investigations. The case could be getting dangerous and he didn't want her in trouble. He could handle himself, but Emma would impulsively and blindly enter into a threatening situation without any consideration for her own safety.

There was little in the background check on Arthur Speigle. Originally from Michigan, he always joked about being glad to have escaped the woods of Michigan for the safety of Manhattan. But that was all Max knew. It was past time to find out more. "Leave this alone," he said to Emma.

"But I want to help," she insisted.

"I don't need your help," he said firmly. This little incident only proved once again that he had to stay far away from Emma Delaney. "I never did."

Her eyes widened and the color drained from her face. He turned around and walked out.

HE'D NEVER NEEDED Emma's help.

He still desired her. He'd loved her once, but their time together had been a brief mistake. One he'd corrected. When he'd been Max Thorne he'd been weak. He'd given in to his passions, his needs too easily. Whatever he'd wanted he'd taken.

Just like he'd almost done tonight. He'd wanted to continue touching Emma, to kiss her, to tell her...what? There was nothing he could tell her. But he couldn't get the damn woman out of his head.

No, he wasn't going to give in to this weakness.

It wasn't until prison forced him to take responsibility for his actions that he'd begun to change. It had been hard, but he was proud of who he was. The work that he did was good work. He helped people, quietly, unobtrusively. He tried to steer them toward the right path, to take responsibility, but he also let them make their own decisions.

The damn case, however, was getting to him. He turned down Fifth Avenue heading toward Central Park, away from his apartment. That weak part of him was urging him to run. To escape. He fought down the urge, but he couldn't fight down his desire for Emma. The woman had him bewitched. Surely it was only because Meg—his stable, solid Meg—was away. A beggar stopped him and he gave the fellow a couple of dollars.

"Hey, man!" The vagrant breathed foul alcohol fumes into his face. "Whatever's eating you up can't be that bad. Have a drink." He offered his brown paper bag. Max declined and stepped around the bum. He was sick of all the nutty people at Scorpion Books. And of the Coopers' blind allegiance to Jay.

He knew better. He knew the real nature of people. People were weak. People gave in to their base desires. To their weaknesses. Their needs.

He was a prime example.

He'd fought against his own nature—in fact he'd thought he'd won—but no matter how hard he tried he couldn't deny what he really was.

The moon cast a weak shadow along Park Avenue as he approached the exclusive apartment building. Now that he'd decided not to fight his true nature he picked up the pace, nodding at the doorman, punching the floor number in the elevator. It was past time he admitted it to himself. He was Max Thorne. A man who took what he wanted and damn the consequences.

He'd done it eight years ago when he'd met Emma. She'd been younger then, but even more, she'd been sweeter, more trusting. He was the one who had changed all that.

He rang the apartment's doorbell.

True, Emma had thrown herself at him that night, but he'd known what he was doing. He'd wanted her from the moment he'd seen her and had fallen in love almost as quickly.

He was afraid he'd never fallen out of love.

The door opened and she said, "Max!"

"Yes," he answered. He stepped inside, closed the door behind him and pulled Emma into his arms. "Say it again." His voice came out husky and he heard the need. With one hand on the small of her back, the other cupping her head, he lowered his face to hers. But she held him away, pressing her hands against his chest.

"What?" she asked, confused, but he also felt her melting against him. It had always been like this between them. He remembered everything. He was tired of pretending, of denying who he really was.

"My name. Say my name. Max," he breathed against her lips, letting his hands settle on her hips. Emma felt so right in his arms. He needed to hear her say his name, his real name.

"Max," she said, and he kissed her.

Max kissed her as if his life depended on it. He tasted her and she sighed into his mouth. He took possession, claiming her as his woman. She melted against him, opening up to him, and he felt *right* for the first time in a long time. Her lips were sweet and tangy, soft yet firm. He touched and tasted, stroked and teased. Kissing Emma was like discovering a long-lost treasure chest.

She kissed him back passionately, touching his face, his hair as if she couldn't believe it was him. Long moments passed as they kissed, touched, rediscovered each other.

Suddenly Emma stilled and then pushed away from him. Max loosened his hold on her, allowing her to put inches between them, but he didn't let go. He didn't think he could.

"Max," she said, puzzled at first, and then added more firmly, "Max, what are you doing?"

"I'm kissing you. And I intend to do a lot more." He lowered his lips to her mouth, but Emma moved her face. That didn't deter him. He explored her cheek, the soft skin of her neck. He moved his mouth along her jaw and nibbled on her ear—she'd always enjoyed that. Emma sighed, leaned into him and then used her arms to push against his shoulders.

"Max, we shouldn't be doing this."

He was past any logical arguments. His body was demanding to join with hers and he wanted to discover if sex with Emma really was as good as he remembered. He stopped kissing her and looked at her. "You're alone, aren't you?"

Emma nodded.

"I've locked the door."

"Yes, but—"

He scooped her up in his arms and headed toward the bedroom. "Max," she protested again, and he stopped her words with a kiss that ended only when he had her next to the bed.

"It's a pretty blouse." He touched her white silk blouse and then began to undo the buttons. Words were inadequate for what he was feeling, and he was afraid to tell her, anyway. He still wasn't sure exactly what he was feeling.

She looked at him, her blue eyes filled with desires and questions. "Max?"

He had her blouse undone and he drew it down her arms, kissing each shoulder blade as it was uncovered for his hungry eyes.

"Max. We...I don't think...this is such a good idea."

He held one finger against her lips. There was absolutely no way he'd be able to let Emma go tonight. "Let's not talk."

"But we always used to talk so well."

"It was all lies," he said, removing his shirt. He touched her breast, his large hand dark against her soft, white skin. "This was never a lie."

Emma gasped as he cupped her breasts together, then unhooked her bra, freeing her. He lowered his mouth, first sucking on a nipple and then grazing it with his teeth.

"No." Emma grabbed his head between her hands, pulling him away. He let her, raising his head to hers. "We shouldn't. This is wrong." But he saw that her face was flushed with desire. He knew the conflict she was feeling, but he also knew that she was fighting a losing battle.

"Is it? Isn't this where we've been heading for the last week? Isn't this why you continued to tease me every day? Reminding me of what it used to be like between us?"

"Tease you? That's offensive. I may have wanted to annoy you, make you pay a little for what you did to me," Emma admitted in her incredibly honest manner, "but I thought you were the one who had all the control. Your much vaunted *control.*" Her eyes flashed angrily and she grabbed him by the shoulders, pressing him against the bed, pushing him onto his back. Like a warrior princess she towered above him, holding his arms, her blouse undone, her breasts naked.

He grinned. He couldn't help it, she looked so beautiful. "You're beautiful."

"Beautiful!" She hit him on the shoulder. "What a stupid thing to say at a time like this."

"You are beautiful. I've never ever met anyone like you." He freed his hands from hers and ran them under her blouse along her bare back. She shivered and Max encouraged her to lower herself onto him. Her bare chest against his.

"Oh, Max, now what?" Her words were a soft whisper against his chest.

He held her against his heart, knowing exactly what she meant, but not wanting to talk about it. "Now we do exactly what we've wanted to do since we laid eyes on each other again." He rolled her over, pinning her under him, and kissed her. He continued to kiss her mouth as he unbuckled her belt, unzipped her skirt. Pulling it down, he swept his fingers along her leg to her silk panties, then curved his hand around her hip.

"You still have all your clothes on and I'm practically naked," Emma complained, and she pushed him off of her, attacking his clothes. He remembered how she'd always been in such a hurry to get him naked, she'd ruined several shirts that way. He helped and soon he was naked, while Emma still wore the little panties.

They stopped for a moment, raised on their knees facing each other.

"My, my," she said, "my memory certainly didn't fail me when it came to remembering you." Emma ran a teasing hand down his chest and stomach, lightly trailing her fingers along his shaft. He sucked in his breath and moved involuntarily, pressing himself more firmly into her hand. She held him and then stroked him, very very slowly and then a little harder and a little faster. She smiled a wicked smile. "I think you remember me, too."

He couldn't take any more, so pulled her against him and kissed her once more, his hands cupping her buttocks, caressing them, moving her against him. It was glorious touching her again, kissing her again, remembering what pleased her, making her want him.

"Max, not so fast." Emma kissed him on his jaw and then his neck, and he wondered why he had resisted her for so long. She bent her head and kissed his nipples. "Remember how you used to like this?" she asked as she pressed her nipples against his and then rubbed her naked breasts against his chest.

He closed his eyes and tried to breathe. "Like" was an understatement, he thought as the blood rushed through his veins. All he could smell was Emma's musky scent and skin and sweat and desire. He licked her neck, wanting to consume her. Now that he'd found her, he could never let her go. Moving lower, he cupped her breasts in his hands, petting and stroking as her breathing grew more and more rapid, and then he began to kiss them. Around and around one breast, occasionally touching the nipple lightly with his tongue.

"Now, Max. Please. Like you used to." Emma's voice came out in a gasp.

He took as much of her breast into his mouth as he could, sucking hard, and then repeated his actions on the other plump breast. He pressed her back down on the bed so he could kiss her everywhere he'd been dreaming of. The curves of her soft stomach, her smooth thighs, the back of her knee. He lost himself in the beauty of her body. This was Emma. His Emma.

Emma giggled. "Max, that's not fair. You know my weaknesses."

"Yes I do." He raised himself above her, looking his fill at her pretty, pink flushed body. He slowly dragged off the panties, then trailed his hand slowly, ever so slowly, back up her leg along the inner thigh, watching her eyes grow bigger and bigger until he brushed against her curls.

He kissed her hard on the mouth, his tongue thrusting into her mouth in strong stroking motions as his fingers entered her, repeating the actions. Emma bucked against him, but Max wouldn't allow her to move, keeping her trapped with the weight of his body on hers. Finally he let her tear her mouth away. "Max, you're driving me wild. I need you."

"Say that again." He wanted to hear the words over and over again.

"Max, I need you. Now."

Max poised himself above Emma and entered her with his body, his hands framing her face, their eyes locked as their bodies joined. Once he'd entered her, he held himself completely immobile. For a few moments, they simply gazed at each other.

Then he began to rock his hips and Emma wrapped her slender legs around his waist and joined his rhythm. He wanted to kiss her and touch her, but he couldn't. All he could do was concentrate on where their bodies joined, how he'd never expected this to happen again and how he never wanted it to end. But even as he thought that, he realized he was moving faster, climbing higher and he couldn't hold back. He heard Emma cry out and shudder as she came and then he joined her in the mindless descent. Out of control.

10

The morning after

EMMA TRAILED HER HAND along Max's chest and he moved slightly against her. "Stop that," he complained softly, "I'm too tired."

She rested her head against his shoulder and he wrapped his arms around her. "This is nice," she murmured.

"Mmm," he responded sleepily.

She elbowed him. "Don't fall asleep." He didn't stir so she grazed his stomach lightly with her fingertips, tickling him where she knew he was sensitive.

"Witch," he growled as he rolled over on top of her, capturing her wrists in his hands and pinning them down on the mattress. At least she had his full attention, and from the feel of his body pressed against her, it wasn't only his mind that was aware of her. He wanted her again and her body responded. She was afraid she would never be tired of him.

"Emma," he said, his brown eyes dark, intense. He studied her and she couldn't keep the happiness from her face. As Max continued to look at her, she saw a multitude of emotions cross his own face, then he frowned. Suddenly he rolled off her, got out of bed and reached for his clothes.

She shivered, feeling cold and afraid. Their lovemaking had been so incredible. When he'd arrived so unexpectedly at her door and pulled her into his arms, she couldn't believe what was happening. She'd managed to convince herself that the love that she and Max had once shared was dead.

His cold words to her earlier this evening had convinced her of that fact, but now their lovemaking had proved a different story. Hadn't it?

With dread, she watched Max pull on his pants, his shirt, and begin looking for his tie without saying a word to her. She couldn't believe he was thinking of leaving. He wouldn't dare. Not without talking about what had happened! About what it meant. About their future. About Meg...

Feeling naked all at once, she pulled up the sheet to cover her breasts and sat up in bed, watching Max wrap his tie around his neck. She noted with satisfaction that he stuffed his underwear into his pocket. Good, he wasn't nearly as unaffected as he was pretending. "What are you doing?" She was pleased at how cool and sophisticated her voice sounded. Inside she was dying.

"Getting dressed." He kept his back to her, moving methodically, as if she meant nothing to him.

"But..." she began, and didn't know what else to say. She almost expected his next words.

Max faced her, his expression blank. "We got that out of our system. Now we can move on."

He might pretend all he wanted, but she saw the pulse at his throat pounding furiously. Emma refused to believe his words. She picked up one of the lacy, Victorian pillows, put it down, found her wind-up travel alarm clock and threw it at him. Max ducked, the clock crashed into the wall and fell in a shattered heap to the floor.

"Don't you dare say this was just sex."

"It was," he said coldly. "Just *sex.* An itch that needed to be scratched. And as you've taken such pains to remind me, I have been without a woman for too long. A man can be celibate for only so long."

Max began to pace, refusing to meet her eyes, and she knew he was lying. "Emma, I never meant to hurt you, but we do have a history, a very passionate history, and this—"

he gestured at the rumpled bed ''—well, it was almost inevitable. But we're adults and we can get past this...this lust.''

"How dare you! Are you telling me that since you got me out of your system, you're going to wait for sex until your wedding night?" As soon as the word *wedding* was out of her mouth, they both froze.

The great guilt god whomped Emma hard over the head. She realized exactly how Max was feeling. She'd betrayed her friend; he'd betrayed his fiancée. "Oh no. We made love in Meg's apartment. In Meg's bed.'' Meg's romantic, antique four-poster covered in ivory and cream. A bed Emma would have loved to have for herself. Instead, look at what she had done. She couldn't have just bought a bed identical to her friend's. No, she had to bed Meg's man.

"*Sex.* We had sex,'' Max insisted almost desperately.

"Whatever word you want to use, we betrayed Meg,'' Emma responded angrily. "Now what?"

Max ran a hand through his dark hair and faced her. Her heart clutched at the pain on his face. "Nothing. We do *nothing.* We stay away from each other. If you have questions about the wedding, send me an E-mail.''

"Are you afraid of me? Of us?" She knew she was pushing him, but she couldn't help herself. She wondered what she wanted. For Max to declare his undying love for her? To suggest that they run away together this very minute?

Max took a last look around the room, probably checking for a cuff link or some other piece of incriminating evidence. He tucked his shirt in his pants, buttoned his jacket. "No. I'm not afraid. I don't want to insult you, but I have you out of my system.''

He took a step toward her and then stopped. "I'm sorry." He left.

Emma watched in shock as Max disappeared. She wished this was her apartment so she could break as many objects as she wanted. She wished she could pack her bags this very instant and flee back to Philadelphia, back to her comfortable, safe life. Her life, however, would never be the same now that Max had reentered it. He was going to break her heart again.

What was she going to do?

OUT OF HIS SYSTEM, HA! It had taken Emma a restless night, a morning spent slamming through the apartment, berating herself for being a fool, before the truth hit her.

As she was walking to Scorpion Books, she realized it: Max was scared.

He had feelings for her, she knew. Asking her to call him Max showed he hadn't gotten over their past any more than she had.

But what exactly did she want? What did she think she was doing? What did she want Max to do?

What about Meg?

Emma stopped stock-still at a red light, dizzy from the questions assaulting her, until an annoyed pedestrian nudged her out of the way so he could jaywalk like any decent New Yorker would.

Exactly what was she, Emma Grace Delaney, caught up in? A big mess. And she had helped create it by constantly needling Max, bringing up their past, testing their sexual attraction. Last night she'd gotten exactly what she'd asked for. And she could no longer deny what she wanted.

She wanted Max Thorne. For herself. Forever.

How could she? How could she betray her friend and pull Max onto a path he was desperate to stay away from? That was why he'd said those cutting words last night and left.

She knew another truth as well, one she'd been trying to ignore: she loved him.

That stopped her again, except this time she quickly ducked into a coffee shop. With all these moments of self-revelation, she needed to sit down. Finding a booth, she ordered bacon and eggs—her appetite had suddenly returned and cholesterol was the least of her worries.

She loved Maxwell Thorne. She'd never stopped loving him. That was sobering. Once she was in love it looked like it stuck.

What about Meg? Deep down Emma didn't believe that Meg loved Max nearly as much as she did. Meg hadn't jumped to defend Max as she had. Meg was more concerned over the future of Scorpion Books than her future with Max.

Max belonged to Emma.

But what was she willing to do about it? Surely she didn't want to put Meg through the same pain and embarrassment Emma had suffered eight years ago?

The waitress dropped off the breakfast and Emma asked for a side order of pancakes. She had a lot of thinking to do.

BACK AT THE PUBLISHING offices, Emma called Beth and the aunts to confirm the colors of the tablecloths and napkins. With only days to the wedding, she was glad for their help, especially since she was so confused emotionally. Then Jill came in, dressed in a peasant skirt and blouse and hoop earrings that would have made a gypsy proud. She began by asking a number of questions about wedding customs. Emma was worried that Jill wanted to query her about her relationship with Max—she'd like to know the answers to those questions herself—but Jill continued her interview about wedding folklore. With only half her attention on the subject—thoughts of Max were still scrambling her brain— Emma detailed different traditions and some of the more unusual weddings she had organized.

"You do know a lot about the various traditions."

"It's my hobby. I like to be able to incorporate ethnic and historical touches."

"Hmm, yes," Jill said. "You say you used to work as a publicist, writing press releases and such."

"Yes, I did." Emma waited, wondering where Jill was headed.

Jill fingered one of her earrings and then said, as if the thought had just occurred to her, "Have you ever thought of writing a book?"

"A book? I couldn't."

"Sure you could. *Have Wedding Dress, Will Travel* is a great title. I can already see it on the nonfiction bestseller lists."

"Don't you need more than a title?" Emma asked, more than a little bewildered. Jill was moving ahead so quickly.

"A title is important because so much of publishing is marketing these days. And I'm very, very good at marketing. And at recognizing an idea that could sell." Jill stopped her rush of words and took a deep breath. "I realize I've surprised you, but ever since everyone at Scorpion has gotten so caught up with wedding fever, I haven't been able to stop thinking about the possibilities. If you put together a chatty book filled with wedding trivia, advice and stories of weddings you've planned, we'd both have a bestseller on our hands." Jill stood. "Think about it. I'd be willing to help you put together an outline and pitch it to the editorial committee." She stared hard at Emma. "My only requirement is that you give me the book and not Meg. I approached you first."

"I don't know what to say."

"Just say you'll think about it and give the book to me." Jill left while Emma gaped. Jill Ellis was very good at her job. Determined and ambitious, wanting to best her lover's daughter. Could she be ruthless enough to be the thief?

Editors really were an odd breed.

Just as Emma was wondering if she could write a book, if she wanted to write a book, Jay walked into Emma's office. "What should I do about Sarah?" He looked panicked. "I really need your help. You're the bridal expert and everything I've done has backfired."

"Including whatever you were doing in her office two nights ago. Tell me," Emma begged, seizing the opportunity.

"Not you too, Emma. Frasier has everyone convinced of my guilt and he's the one with a criminal record." Jay sank into a chair, burying his face in his hands.

Emma walked over to him and put her own hands on his shoulders. "You're probably asking the wrong person for help with your love life," she said wryly, considering her own predicament. "Remember, I'm the bridal consultant whose groom abandoned her at the altar!" If she wrote a book, then the whole world would know about her sorry past. Now that she knew she was still in love with Max—and had no idea what was going to happen between them—could her poor pride take another beating?

When Jay didn't say anything Emma sighed and sat down next to him. Surely she could give Jay some useful advice out of all her own mistakes. "Have you told Sarah how you feel about her?"

"She knows."

"No, I mean been totally honest and told her. Told her why it's Sarah you love and not someone else." Should Emma do the same with Max? Tell him she loved him?

Jay considered her question and then his face lit up. "Because she's wonderful. It's like I found the part of myself that was missing. She doesn't care who my father is or what schools I went to, but she laughs at my jokes. We can be at a deadly dull business affair, but if I catch her eye, I know she can tell what I'm thinking." Jay smiled. "Plus she's so confident. She knows who she is—probably because she had to do it all herself. When I bring a smile to her face, I feel like I've accomplished more than I did during all of the rest of my life."

Emma was overwhelmed by how passionately Jay felt for Sarah. "Then tell her that. Tell her exactly how you feel. She won't know for sure until you do." Is that what *she* needed to do? Emma wondered again.

"Maybe you're right," Jay said. "Thanks. This being in love business, really in love, is a lot more complicated than most of us guys ever imagine. I dated a lot of women before Sarah and thought I was in love once or twice before, but nothing like this. I think that's why I'm so scared now. But you're right, I don't have anything to lose." He took her hand and squeezed it. "Emma, I care about you. I used to have a crush on you when I was a kid. And, well...you're spending an awful lot of time with Frasier."

Emma knew she turned bright red.

"No," Jay interrupted before she could do more than open her mouth. "I'm not claiming you're trying to steal Meg's fiancé, although if you were I think I'd help. I wish Meg was more desperate to marry him. I wish she was more in love with him. But what do we really know about Frasier Thorne? Why am I the only one suspicious of his motives?"

"Oh, Jay, he's a good man. You have to believe me."

"You keep saying that. Meg keeps saying that. Why am I so afraid that Frasier Thorne is going to bring this family more heartache than we could ever imagine?"

MAX AVOIDED EMMA all day long, and she gave him that time. The office wasn't the best place for her to say what she wanted to say to him, but she wasn't about to let the whole day go by without taking action, either. She was a woman of action, after all. A woman who had turned her wedding humiliation into a business success. She needed to start believing her own press.

But when she went looking for him at six o'clock, he'd left for the evening. Mrs. Daley saw her standing outside his office and smiled grimly. "Mr. Thorne has gone for the day. I believe he had a dinner date."

"Oh, a business dinner," Emma said thankfully.

"No, dear. A personal dinner. I put the call through to him from the young woman. Now perhaps you'll remember he's engaged to Miss Cooper and leave the man alone."

Flummoxed, Emma watched Mrs. Daley smile and then leave. She shivered. Why did that woman dislike her?

Having abandoned the last of her pride, Emma skulked into Max's office and searched his desk for a clue as to where he might be with the young woman. *What young woman?* She was nobody, Emma assured herself. Max hadn't suddenly turned into the playboy of east Manhattan. He was torn up about his betrayal over Meg. That's why he was avoiding her. Not because he'd decided to conquer the female population of New York.

He'd taken his schedule with him, but on his speed dial Emma discovered several restaurants. She telephoned them one by one, checking for a Thorne reservation, and on her fourth call she found him.

L'Étoile was tucked into the corner of a small, old hotel, its dark interior illuminated by soft lights. *Dark and romantic,* she snorted to herself. As the maître d' was seating a couple, Emma ducked into the restaurant and looked around. *Small rooms with intimate, white linen covered tables. Candles. Romantic.*

Having wandered through two small rooms pretending to be looking for the bathroom, she spotted Max and his friend. The woman was beautiful, with straight blond hair pulled back by a velvet bow. She was wearing a soft gray dress that should have done nothing for any female, yet made her skin glow and her eyes sparkle. Emma hated her.

"Max, here you are," Emma said as she approached the table. "I've been looking for you everywhere."

Max stood before he was fully aware of her presence and then he frowned. "What are you doing here?"

"A small wedding crisis." She stressed the word *wedding*.

Then she stuck out her hand. "Hello, I'm Emma Delaney, Mr. Thorne's wedding consultant."

The blond goddess took it, shaking firmly. "Hello, I'm Beverly Austin." A waiter appeared with a chair for Emma.

"Thank you." She sat down. "Nice restaurant."

"I like it," Ms. Beverly Austin agreed. She reached across the table and squeezed Max's hand in a proprietorial manner. "We used to come here a lot when we were dating."

"You and Max—Frasier—used to date?"

"Yes, I can't believe I let him get away. When I found out Frasier was getting married, well, I just had to take him out to dinner to celebrate." The woman batted her eyelashes at Max.

Emma flagged down a waiter. "Vodka martini."

"So you're the bridal consultant," Beverly cooed. "It must be rewarding to work in such a traditionally female occupation. Your mother must be very happy. All that lace and satin and stuff. Of course, when I do the dirty deed I plan to do it very simply and sophisticatedly. A Chanel suit, a few friends."

"Oh, have you found someone to marry?" Emma asked brightly.

"Well, I'm dating a very pleasant man, but we haven't set anything firm yet."

"Perhaps you should try *The Rules*. You might find the chapters on not having sex on the first date especially illuminating. It's on the top of all the bestseller lists." Emma smiled sweetly as Beverly glared.

"What do you do for a living?" Emma asked.

"I'm an investment banker."

"Oh, these cold hard institutions that make so much money off the ordinary person. How do you sleep at night?"

"Very well in my penthouse apartment. And is your little business successful?"

"Fabulously. In fact, I had to turn down Barbra Streisand

and James Brolin," she fibbed furiously. Emma grabbed her drink out of the waiter's hand before he had a chance to place it on the table and took a healthy swig.

"What kind of emergency?" Max finally asked, breaking in.

"What?" Emma asked. "Oh, that. Yes, the emergency. The tuxedo shop got the measurements all wrong for your tux, so I promised to take you there tonight. They agreed to stay open late. Gosh—" she looked at her watch and marveled that the word *gosh* had actually left her mouth "—it's 8:30 now. We'd better rush."

"Why doesn't Frasier wear his own tux?" Beverly asked.

"Because it's a Civil War theme. It's a special Rhett Butler tuxedo."

Max grimaced but remained silent. Beverly looked at him questioningly. "I had hoped we could at least get to the entrée, but if you have to leave..."

"No," he said. "I don't have to leave. Miss Delaney has to leave." He stood and helped Emma to her feet.

"But—but," she stammered as he handed her her purse and briefcase, "at least let me measure you—"

"I don't want to be measured."

"It's important."

"All right." He gave in, a look of resignation on his face. "Let's go to the cloakroom. I won't be more than a minute," he said to Beverly.

"I'll be here," she promised. "I won't make the mistake of letting you go again."

Max practically dragged Emma through the dining room to the cloakroom, not letting go of her arm. "What is your problem?" he demanded when they arrived. "Why are you trying to embarrass me in front of an old friend?"

"Friend, ha! You mean girlfriend."

"Beverly and I had a very nice relationship. Now she's taking me out for a celebratory dinner. Nothing more. Nothing less."

"Max, you can't really believe that. That woman is after you. She's dressed to the teeth to try to win you back. This is her one chance. I bet she just heard you were engaged."

"Well yes, she did say she'd only heard about my engagement yesterday."

"She's a woman of action. She's going to tempt you with every lure she knows. She wants you back."

"Don't put your own feelings onto Beverly. You're the one using every trick you know to win me back!"

Emma was shocked. "You actually think I'm trying to trick you?"

"What do you call this evening's exhibition? Especially after I made my feelings very clear this morning."

"I'm not anything like Beverly. I've been up front about my feelings for you. I've never pretended otherwise. You're the one who's pretending. Pretending that marrying Meg is the right thing to do when you're in love with me."

"I don't love you," Max said firmly.

"Then why did you make love with me?"

"It was sex."

"No, it was love," she said too loudly, and realized the maître d' was frowning toward the cloakroom.

"You're confused, Emma. What we had was eight years ago. It's time you realized that." Max turned around, then stopped and faced her again. "And what we had was *over* eight years ago. Last night confirmed it." He walked away from her. Back to Beverly. Back to the life he had chosen.

Leaving her alone.

11

Girl's night out

AS EMMA WALKED in the door of Meg's apartment the phone was ringing. She rushed to it, hoping it was Max. Maybe he'd regretted the words he'd said to her at the restaurant. She certainly regretted them!

"Is that you, Emma?" Meg's bright voice asked over the phone. "You sound sort of strange."

"I just got in for the evening and ran for the phone."

"You're working late on my wedding. I feel so guilty."

"No," Emma assured her, suddenly realizing that she was speaking to the woman she'd betrayed. The friend she wanted Max to jilt. "Don't feel bad over me. I deserve what I'm getting." Including Max's cold response. A small part of her still hoped he'd show up at the apartment so they could talk and deal with what was going on between then. Surely something *was* going on between them?

"I'm going to be held up another day or two."

Emma didn't know if she was relieved or worried. "Is Zoe Dixon having problems with the book?"

"No, Zoe is on a roll. Her fingers are flying over the keyboard. At least that's how she describes the writing process. It makes me a little nervous, I wish she'd spend some more time thinking, but she is a TV person and we are on deadline. The problem is at the office, the L.A. office of Scorpion. Well, I've uncovered some weird things." Meg's voice sounded strained.

"Is it Jay?"

"Yes."

"Meg, I'm so sorry. It doesn't look good here, either." Emma filled her in on all the strange goings on, including Brenda Lau, Art Spiegle's henchmen and Jay's nocturnal activities.

"I'm so worried about him," Meg confided. "I know that he resented me when we were younger, because I always knew I wanted to be a part of Scorpion Books, while he just sort of drifted. I was so happy when he finally came back and decided to be part of the firm. I thought he'd found his roots, but maybe he was just looking for a way to get back at us. To hurt us as much as we must have hurt him when he was young."

"Meg, I just can't believe that about Jay. I don't think he'd want to disappoint Sarah Tepper."

"Yes. His obvious affection for Sarah is a good sign. But he might have started all the trouble before he fell in love with Sarah and now he doesn't know how to get out. Oh, if it really is him, if he would just tell us, I know Daddy could figure some way out of this trouble, but..."

There was just too much trouble going around, Emma thought.

"I tried calling Frasier earlier tonight," Meg continued. "His machine picked up."

"Oh, he's out for dinner," Emma said before thinking.

"With who?"

"Beverly Austin."

"That old flame." Meg chuckled. "Is she trying to get her claws back into my man?"

"Yes," Emma answered weakly, refusing to wonder what Meg would have to say about herself. Emma Delaney, groom-stealing bridal consultant extraordinaire.

"Poor Frasier. He probably has no idea what he got himself into. I wish I could phone him tonight once he gets home, but I have to go to a TV thing with Zoe Dixon. Maybe you could phone him for me, Emma?"

"No! I mean, I'm really tired and making it an early night. I'll tell him tomorrow at the office that you called."

"Great." Meg chatted for a few minutes more about the peculiarities of L.A. and then hung up.

Emma put on her nightgown, washed her face and brushed her teeth, and then sat on the couch, waiting. Waiting for Max.

She waited a long time and then went to bed alone.

AFTER EMMA LEFT HIM and Beverly, Max was no longer able to concentrate on his dinner or his dining companion. Too soon he discovered that what Emma had claimed was true. In the taxi Beverly made it very clear she'd like to have a chance to make him forget all about his bride-to-be.

He politely walked her to her apartment door and extricated himself from her clutches in as gentlemanly a fashion as possible. Beverly smiled at him sadly. "I hope you won't blame a girl for trying, Frasier. I was a fool to let you go."

"Thank you for the compliment. But I'm getting married in a few days."

"Lucky woman. You must really love her."

"I do," he answered, and told himself he was referring to Meg.

Beverly unlocked her door and walked in. "Good bye, Frasier Thorne. I hope she makes you happy."

Back in the taxi, Max reflected that he didn't need any help forgetting about his bride-to-be. Whenever Emma was in the room, he forgot all about Meg. In the restaurant's cloakroom he'd had an overwhelming urge to kiss Emma, to make some excuse to Beverly and drag Emma off to his apartment and his bed. Their lovemaking had been every bit as good as he'd remembered, and better.

But if he gave in to his weakness again, he'd never be able

to stop. His one night with Emma had been a mistake. One he was never going to repeat. He was never going to hurt Meg. Meg loved him and he'd made her a promise: to love and care for her the rest of his life. He intended to do exactly that.

God, but he felt guilty over Emma.

He'd hoped his...feelings for her were only that of a celibate man who'd spent too much time with a beautiful woman. He'd been trying to prove that theory to himself this evening by spending time with Beverly. When she'd called him, he'd gladly accepted her invitation, hoping to feel an old spark of attraction to her, to prove that he was just a normal man reacting to an attractive woman. That Emma Delaney had the same effect on his equilibrium as any other beautiful woman. That he no longer loved her.

Beverly was beautiful and witty and had made it clear she wanted him, but he'd felt no attraction for her. He'd been hoping he would. If he had, then he'd have known his one night with Emma was just a weakness he'd be able to overcome.

But when he'd felt nothing for Beverly, he'd begun to fear that he might still be in love with Emma Delaney.

No matter what old feelings were stirring within him, he was not a man who broke his promises. He was going to marry Meg Cooper.

Another terrible thought hit him. If he married Meg, would he be hurting Emma? No, that was ridiculous. Emma had made a new life for herself. Being involved with him would only complicate her existence. She might have some lingering attraction for him, might want to punish him for betraying her, but she wasn't really in love with him.

There, that settled it. Emma Delaney was not in love with him and he was definitely not in love with her.

Max prayed that the wedding would hurry and get here.

AFTER A DAY OF ARGUING with the caterer, then finding an extra hundred chairs because Peter Cooper invited everyone from Scorpion Books to come to the reception, Emma had had enough—and she wished she had a shoulder to cry on.

She stopped off at Sarah Tepper's office. At first she thought the office was empty but then she saw a pile of manuscripts move.

"Sarah?"

"Here," came the muffled answer, and Sarah's head rose above the stack. "I'm working on the floor, trying to get through some of my slush. I feel so bad for these poor authors who've had their book just sitting here, waiting and waiting. It's tough on them, but I so rarely have any time to actually read."

"Any chance I can drag you away for dinner?"

"You got it. A girls night out." Sarah smiled, her beautiful face glowing as she left the manuscripts piled on the floor and stood. "We could have fancy drinks and gossip about the groom and absent bride. Or we could discuss our love lives." Her brown eyes flashed. "I know I could use a good chat about Jay. I have no idea what to do about him."

Sarah shook her head as she walked to her desk, picked up her purse and a briefcase overloaded with manuscripts. She smiled ruefully when she saw Emma looking at the latter. "Sometimes I read them on the train or in the bathtub. Mostly they travel with me. I have manuscripts that have journeyed from one end of the country to the other in my book bag and I still haven't read them. Good intentions need to be followed through." She linked her elbow with Emma's. "But tonight I want the bridal expert's opinion on what I should do about Jay. And maybe you'll tell me about the man who's tying your life up in knots."

Emma opened her mouth to issue a denial and then changed her mind. She did want to talk to someone and, intuitively, she knew that Sarah could be a good friend. "Am I that obvious?"

"Transparent as glass to another woman in love," Sarah agreed as she grabbed her coat. "Tell me more once we have a silly drink in front of us."

From the office, they walked two blocks to Moloney's Grill, a new bar and restaurant favored by the publishing industry. They ordered margaritas, the house specialty.

"I'm in love with him," Sarah said, and took a healthy sip. "Men—can't live with 'em, can't have good sex without 'em."

Emma spluttered into her drink when Sarah spoke so clearly the people at the next two tables also heard. "Why won't you give Jay a chance?" she asked when she'd recovered.

"Other than the obvious cultural differences and family backgrounds? What am I going to tell my mother—that I'm in love with a rich, blond WASP? Because he's serious. He claims he wants the lifetime-commitment, rings, forever kind of deal. I was hoping we could just have fun."

Sarah giggled and then hiccupped. Emma sighed. Over gourmet pizza, they shared the sorry details of their sorry love lives. Emma was fairly vague about her man, and as Sarah did most of the talking, she was sure Sarah didn't know that it was Max she was in love with. Heavens, Sarah didn't even know who Max was. This was all too confusing.

Instead, Emma decided to try to help Jay and Sarah—especially after the confidences he had shared with her. "You and Jay are playing reverse roles. It's usually the man who doesn't want to commit."

Sarah frowned. "I know. Do you think I'm being a coward?"

"You said you loved him."

She sighed. "I do."

"Then you're being a coward. If the man I loved was willing to say he loved me and wanted a future with me, I'd be willing to risk anything to be with him."

"Anything?" Sarah asked. "You're exaggerating."

"I'd be willing to do a lot," Emma conceded.

Sarah assessed her with those intelligent, penetrating eyes. "Including stealing Meg's guy."

All the alcohol left Emma's brain as she straightened her spine and met Sarah's steady, assessing gaze. "You know?" she asked.

"It's hard not to with all the tension in the air between you two, but I think I'm the only one who's noticed."

"Mrs. Daley knows something. She's always giving me the evil eye."

"Mrs. Daley has taken a sudden dislike to anyone and everyone who is in love. I wish I knew why.... Oh look, over there. I think our brave warriors have come to rescue us. Maybe they were afraid we'd share too many confidences." Sarah waved. Jay and Max appeared at their table.

Jay leaned down to kiss Sarah on the cheek, just as Sarah moved so that their lips touched and she kissed him. Really kissed him. When it ended, finally, Jay took her hands. "Let's go home," he said to her.

"Yes," she agreed. Flashing a look at Emma, she said, "Might as well make a go of it." Just as quickly they were gone.

"Wow," was all Emma could say.

Max sat across the table from her. "Romance counseling? A veritable Renaissance woman."

"Don't be sarcastic. I'm better at giving advice than following it." They looked at each other and Max was the first to look away. He stood and held out his hand. "Let me walk you home."

Emma nodded in agreement. The last thing she needed was to be mugged. Along the short walk down Park Avenue to the multistoried brownstone, Max said little and she said even less. She wanted to tell him how she felt but she was afraid. Afraid of both what he might say and what he might do. He'd abandoned her once before and she feared he was capable of it again.

Finally Max spoke. "The men with Art Spiegle were a group of artists. They were upset because Art's been slow paying the bills. Many of the department heads have been ignoring invoices, trying to give Peter some more money to leverage with."

"So I was wrong again when I suspected Art Spiegle. That seems to be my pattern these days."

He nodded to her doorman and almost too quickly they were at the door. Emma unlocked it with a hand that shook too much, then turned to face Max.

"May I come in?" he asked.

"Yes, of course," she said nervously, and walked in ahead of him, putting her keys on the small table by the door, hanging up her coat in the closet. Left with nothing to do, she walked into the living room. "Can I get you a drink?"

"Brandy would be nice."

She stopped for a minute, unable to remember where Meg kept the liquor.

"I'll get it," Max said, reminding her that he knew Meg's home better than she did. She might be wrong about everything, she decided. She sat down on the couch and waited for Max.

He sat down next to her. Before he could say anything, she hurriedly began. "About your dinner with that woman..."

"Beverly Austin."

"I'm sorry I interrupted like I did, but she was making a play for you."

"You're right, she did. I was surprised. But why did you care?"

"Oh, Max, I'm so sorry, but the truth is that even after all

his time, well, I'm afraid I'm still in love with you." Emma
roze after the words escaped her. How would he react?

"No, you're not," he said with what sounded like horror.

"I am. I love you."

Max sat back as if he'd been hit, and Emma rather suspected he had been. All this time he'd been doing the right
hing because he didn't want to break Meg's heart, and now
Emma had revealed her own feelings.

"I'm sorry for what I said the other night," he said finally.
'I didn't mean it, about getting you out of my system. During all these years, I've never forgotten you. Or what we
vere like. Sometimes the idea of how good we were, how
happy we were is what kept me going when I was in prison
nd convinced I was an utter failure."

"Max." She caressed his cheek, pretending to give comfort
o him but really needing to touch him. "That's the nicest
hing anyone has ever said to me." She burst into tears.

"Emma." Max looked distressed. "Don't cry."

She couldn't stop, and when he turned and pulled her into
his arms she went gratefully. This was the last time Max was
going to hold her, she told herself, and began to cry even
harder.

"Emma, sweatheart, please," he whispered against her
ar.

"When you left me, after the wedding, I cried for two
veeks." She felt him still against her and she pulled her face
out of his jacket. "Oh, look, I'm ruining your suit."

"Don't worry about it," he said harshly. "Is that true?"

She raised her tear-filled eyes to his stormy ones and tried
o put on a brave face. She shouldn't be burdening him so.
Yes, but I'm a big girl. I've survived."

"Oh God, I'm sorry." He gave her his pocket handker-
hief.

Emma accepted it and blew her nose, then tried to wipe
er face. Max took the handkerchief and did it for her.

"Thanks." She smiled weakly, backing away from him a little on the couch. "Maybe it would be a good idea if you left. Imagine what it would look like if Meg walked in right now."

At Meg's name Max's face darkened and he moved farther away from her. Part of Emma was sorry, and part of her was telling her to do the right thing. He looked at her but she had no idea what he was looking for. Finally he stood and took his coat from the back of the couch. "Good night," he said, and walked to the door.

Emma stood and followed him. "Good night," she said softly, realizing she was also saying goodbye. This really was the end for herself and Max. She loved him but he loved Meg. Meg and Frasier would probably have a good life together. She needed to get on with her own. Max opened the door and Emma had to stop herself from physically gasping at the ache she felt. It wasn't fair to lose the same man twice. But this time she'd never had him, she reminded herself.

What they'd had was sex. Nothing more.

Emma vowed to begin a new life as soon as she returned home to Philadelphia. She would go on every blind date her friends suggested. She'd find someone she could be happy with. She wasn't going to spend another eight years pining for a man she couldn't have.

Max closed the door and then bowed his head against it as if in pain. He slammed his fist against the structure and Emma jumped.

"Max?" she asked tentatively, as her heart began to pound too fast.

He turned around, threw his coat on the ground and said, "Come here," his eyes glittering brightly as if he was feverish.

Without thinking, she moved to him and he pulled her into his arms, kissing her softly, gently on the mouth. "I lied," he mumbled against her lips. "It was never just sex between us. From the first moment I saw you, I remembered everything and I began to feel again. Oh God, Emma. I want you so much."

"Max," was all she could say as she held his wonderful face in her palms, staring at his beautiful eyes. "Max, I love you." When she saw him freeze, try to turn into stone in front of her, she pressed herself against him and kissed him. Really kissed him. She had him for now and she wasn't about to let go. She was going to show him how she felt about him.

He was everything she'd ever wanted. In his strong, powerful arms she lost herself completely. Felt only the need to taste and touch him. Her lips teased and stroked, exploring and remembering. She satisfied her need to feel his skin as her hands ran up and down his chest. Her fingers couldn't work on the buttons on his shirt and in desperation she grabbed his lapels and pulled with all her might. Buttons popped and she lowered her lips to his bare chest.

"Damn woman, you're going to be the death of me yet."

Max stood still as she moved her attentions from one masculine nipple to the other, then moved her lips lower. At his belt buckle she blew softly along the trail of dark hair that arrowed beneath it and she felt his abdominal muscles clench. She could no longer stop; instead she fell to her knees. She was intoxicated by his scent. By her desire. By her need to know he wanted her as much as she wanted him.

Emma lowered his zipper and eyed the bulge in his white Jockey briefs with satisfaction. Very gently, she used one finger to outline him, and Max groaned. She looked up at him and saw that he'd closed his eyes, his jaw clenched. "Do you want me to?" she asked softly.

"Yes," he muttered. "I want your mouth on me."

Emma had freed his shaft before Max had finished speaking and in her hand she held him, strong and velvet. Again she ran a finger along him to the tip, where a bead of liquid had escaped. With her tongue she licked it off, and he shuddered. She blew her hot breath on his skin and then let her tongue follow. When she was quite sure he was reaching the breaking point she took him into her mouth, wanting to show him how much she wanted him.

His hands grabbed her head and he pulled her away from him and to her feet. She lost control of their lovemaking as he crushed his mouth over hers, their tongues dueling; as his hands reached under her skirt and pulled down her hose and panties. His mouth left hers as he freed one of her legs. Then, with her panty hose still dangling from her other ankle, he picked her up, wrapping her legs around his waist, and entered her. She wound her arms around his shoulders and clenched him tightly inside her. They gasped together at her action and Emma felt her shoulders touch the back of the door.

She barely noticed the hardness of the wood as Max began to thrust into her. She was trapped between him and the wall, unable to direct any of their actions. All she could do was feel pleasure as their bodies moved together, searching for release.

"Max," she gasped, but she didn't know what she wanted to say.

"Give me everything," he demanded as he controlled her, moving her up and down, and then he held her still and began to love her harder and faster.

"More," she said, as she felt the sweat course down her back. She felt the tension coil within her, tighter and tighter. She was so close to release she couldn't stand it for another minute longer, and then the explosion hit her. She cried out. She heard him shout her name as he emptied himself into her in his own climax.

As their breathing began to still—she had no idea how much later—Max pulled out of her and let her slide down until her feet touched the floor. Her legs wobbled and Max held her against him. "It's okay," he whispered against her hair. "I have you."

Emma tried to pull her senses together as she realized what she and Max had done. Again. He did have her. He had complete control over their relationship. She stepped away from him and looked down at her panties and hose twisted around her foot. She still had one shoe on. Stepping away from him, she removed the shoe and undergarments. Not sure what else to do, she put the latter in her pocket and then looked at Max. He'd straightened his clothes, although his shirt was still undone.

"We need to talk," he said.

"Yes," she agreed, a little afraid of his grim expression. He wasn't going to tell her he loved her.

"This has got to stop."

She hung her head. What had she expected him to say?

"I don't seem able to master myself when I'm around you. God, I'm sorry, Emma."

"Don't say that!" she cried, taking out her anger at herself on him. He bent down and picked up his suit jacket and put it on. He was going to leave.

He looked around the apartment, as if searching for what to say to her. Finally he met her gaze. "We have to stop this. You've proven you can seduce me. But I've worked hard to be a very different man from the one you fell in love with. I'm not the Max you once loved."

"Is that what you think this is about? My form of...revenge?" Emma made herself be strong and not cry.

"That's all it can be. You don't love me. You just wanted to prove a point. And you have. I don't seem to be the kind of man who can stay loyal to any woman."

"Max, that's not what this is about at all. I know you're a different man. But I do have to ask you, do you want me or Meg?"

Before he could answer, Emma heard a key in the door. They turned in horror as Meg walked in.

12

For better or for worse

"GOOD, I WAS HOPING I'd catch the two of you two together," Meg said as she breezed into her apartment.

Emma gaped at her with what she was sure was guilt written all over her face. She dared to glance at Max, but his face was impassive. He reached past her, brushing his arm against her, and she flinched as he took Meg's suitcase. "Darling, you're back earlier than we expected."

"Yes." Meg put down her briefcase and walked into Max's arms. "Hold me for a minute. I'm so tired."

As Max put his arms around his fiancée, he looked at Emma briefly, his eyes dark with worry. God, what had she done to him? He loved Meg, no matter how much she tried to tell herself otherwise. She was the one who was trying to ruin what Max and Meg had together, like a jealous stepsister insisting on shoving her ugly foot into a shoe that didn't fit. Frasier and Meg had a future. A life. They had a happy ending.

Emma decided to leave them alone and put on a pot of coffee in the kitchen. Once she was in the kitchen, though, she had to grasp the counter to stand upright. It hurt to the bone. She felt tears prickle the back of her eyes but she made herself firm up. She found the coffee and measured out the spoonfuls, put water in the pot and pulled out cups and milk and sugar.

No more silly fantasies. It was time to face the damage that her silly dreams of love were creating. She wouldn't blame Max for his brief fling with her. A fling—that's all it had been. He'd always known their relationship was over; now it was her turn to accept this reality.

She was the one who'd always believed that love won. That love conquered all. Well, that was exactly what was happening. Only she was the one who didn't fit into the equation. Max and Meg were in love.

She poured the coffee into Meg's cups, put them on Meg's tray and went back into Meg's living room to face Meg and her groom. The engaged couple had their heads close together over papers spread on the table. Emma stood there holding the tray, unnoticed by them, unable to say anything, afraid she might cry. Max finally saw her and cleared a spot on the glass top.

"Thanks, Emma. I really need this." Meg took a cup and drank. She searched her hair for a pencil and then saw one on the table. She began to tap it against the side of her cup. "The plane ride back was awful. I've always loved planes— I always pretend I'm off on some kind of adventure, that anything might happen to me—but this time I kept thinking about what I had learned and then I just wanted to cry."

Emma sat down. "What did you find?"

"Records. Paper records that had been shipped by accident to our L.A. office. Or rather, their arrival was supposed to look like an accident, but now I think they were sent there on purpose. I was leaving yesterday when Gary Watson remembered them and wondered if I would take them back to New York with me. Naturally, I agreed and didn't think much more of it. But Zoe had practically chained herself to her computer and didn't want me to read any farther until she finished, so I glanced through my manuscript bag for something to read, came across the files and decided to take a look at them." She ran out of breath and stared into space, as if remembering how pleasant her world had been before she'd found the evidence.

She buried her face in her hands. "I can't believe it." She blew her nose, took several deep breaths and smiled weakly at Emma. "At first it just looked like a lot of art invoices, requisitions for payments, nothing unusual. I'd decided it was a batch of invoices that got put into a courier pouch by accident. But then I got curious." She shrugged. "Always a bad habit of mine, being curious. Never being able to leave well enough alone. I'd never really looked at all the sign-offs, the approvals, on a cover before. One of my books, a police procedural by D. C. Hatfield, was included, so I decided to follow it through all the steps. It was fascinating, the art director's initial concept, the designer's suggestions, the artist's sketch, the marketing department's okay for foil and embossing...and I'm telling you all kind of things you don't need to know. Well, as I was getting absorbed, I noticed Jay had signed out the files one night and returned it the next morning."

Meg took another sip of her coffee. "Since he's spent most of his time learning all about the company and a lot of time in marketing, his signature wasn't strange, but I did begin to wonder. At this point, only production people should be handling the film. I kept looking through the other papers and, well, Jay's signature was there—not all the time, but too often."

"But I don't understand," Emma said. "Why only on those documents? Why hasn't Frasier found any such evidence here?"

"Because they were old invoices. Over a year old. Before any investigation began. Before my father even realized that somebody was stealing."

"So Jay hid the evidence by sending it to L.A.?"

"It's a good way to hide evidence and if it's found, it would just seem like a mistake."

"Why didn't he destroy the papers? Then there would be no evidence at all." Despite everything Max had told her, despite what Meg had discovered, Emma still found it difficult to believe Jay was guilty.

Meg shook her head. "He probably wasn't thinking very clearly. Whatever made him nervous made him act quickly, and he got the evidence as far away from Daddy as possible."

"But I still don't understand," Emma continued. "Why hasn't Frasier found anything in his investigation?"

Max shook his head. "I have." He frowned. "I've found something very similar. It's possible Jay has become more sophisticated. Learned to hide his tracks much better. His first instinct was panic, but then he recovered. I've traced some old cover film as well, but it took me weeks to get there. Since I found it, I've been trying to confirm that it really is Jay and not someone else setting him up."

Meg wiped at the tears rolling down her cheeks, but she managed to make her voice fairly steady. "I still can't believe it. I can't believe Jay would betray the people he loved."

"People you love can hurt you in all kinds of ways," Max said quietly. He took Meg's hand. "Meg, I have to tell you something." He looked at Emma, resolute, and Emma realized he was about to tell Meg everything. About their past, about what had gone on while Meg was away.

Meg put her hand over his. "What is it? I don't think I could take any more bad news."

Emma leaned forward and knocked Meg's coffee cup into her lap.

Meg jumped up. "I'm so sorry," Emma exclaimed. "Your skirt, it's covered with coffee. You'd better change into something else before it stains." She offered her cloth napkin to Meg, who dabbed at her skirt, but the spot got bigger.

"Damn. I've got some club soda in the kitchen. Excuse me while I change."

As soon as Meg was out of the room, Emma turned on Max, "You can't tell her!"

"I have to. I can't marry her after what we—"

"You love her. She loves you. What we had was a crazy, stupid fling."

"Don't say that, Emma. You're right. What we had eight years ago isn't completely dead. I was afraid of the feelings between us. I should have believed in us then—"

"No," she interrupted, realizing that he might be saying what she'd wanted to hear for a long time, what she'd wanted to hear until Meg had arrived, but that it wasn't right. "What we had eight years ago died. I may have been deluding myself and I'm sorry if you began to believe me. But I don't love you anymore. It was nothing more than old feelings."

"Emma, you're lying."

"No, for the first time, I'm really telling the truth. You and Meg belong together. Look how she came to you for comfort and for help after she found the latest evidence. She believes in you, Max. Don't ruin it by telling her about this stupid, stupid time between us. It didn't mean anything."

He looked like he wanted to say something, but Meg came back into the room and into his arms. She wrapped her arms around him and he slowly put his around her. Emma wanted to leave. Her heart was breaking, but if she left now, Max might not believe her. And for his happiness and Meg's, he had to believe her.

Because she'd finally realized what love was all about. It was about being willing to sacrifice your own happiness for the happiness of the one you loved. What Max had been willing to do eight years ago. And what she had to do now.

It was only four days to the wedding. She would try to stay in the background as much as possible. And once the ceremony was over, once Meg and Max said "I do," Emma would leave as quickly and quietly as possible. And she wouldn't be back—not until they'd had at least two children and she was married herself.

"Oh, Frasier," Meg said, as she removed herself from his embrace. "I was rather hoping I'd have an adventure in L.A., but I didn't like it at all."

"Maybe Jay isn't guilty," Max finally said.

"What?" the two women said in unison, looking at him in puzzlement.

"It's too easy. The evidence pointing to Jay is just waiting for someone to find it. I'm beginning to think that if you hadn't found the documents, something else incriminating would have shown up very soon."

"But I don't understand," Meg said. "You were always the one who thought Jay was responsible for the thefts. Oh, I know you didn't say it out loud to me, but I could see it was what you were thinking."

"I know. You and your father and Emma were the ones who were convinced that it couldn't be him. No matter how potentially bad it looked for him. Because he was family. Because he wouldn't betray you. Well, what I'm beginning to learn is that you have to trust the people you love. And you have to tell them the truth in return." He stopped and looked first at Meg and then at Emma. She could see the conflict and the indecision on his face. She prayed that he'd take the time to think before he did anything rash.

He seemed to make a decision, for his back straightened and he took Meg's hands once again. "I'd never want to do anything to hurt you or your family. You have to believe me."

"I do." Meg looked puzzled as she stared up at him, trying to figure out what he meant.

"Then let me take these papers. I want to do some more checking. I've had an idea for a little while—it was what the aunts said, about who would want to hurt your family. We'll talk again in the morning."

"Of course," Meg said in relief.

Max picked up the papers, stuffed them in his briefcase and said his goodbyes.

Meg kissed him good-night and walked him to the door. When she came back she slumped on the couch next to Emma. "Well, once again my timing seems to be off."

"What?" Emma replied too guiltily.

"Frasier and me. I had rather hoped that we would spend the night together. The last time we spoke on the phone he seemed rather anxious, and I must admit I'm getting more than a little frustrated myself." She took off her shoes and rubbed her toes. "But then I barge in with all this bad news. A real killer for a good sex life."

Emma couldn't agree more.

"But at least this will give you and me a chance to talk and catch up. I can hardly believe that you've been planning my wedding and I've been running around worrying about books as per usual."

"That's okay." Emma was happy to reassure her. "I love what I do."

"Yes, you were always the romantic one. When I heard about your business, I realized that you had found the perfect career for yourself. But tell me." Meg paused. "Is it enough? I mean, you're very successful, but after Max, I've never seen you really serious about a man." She sighed and tapped her pencil against her lips. "I've been thinking about marriage a lot recently."

"Well, that's only natural, as you're about to tie the knot. Frasier is a good man. You've made a good choice."

"Yes, I think so, but...it's just confusing. Everything that's been happening with our company and Jay and the wedding. I had a lot of time to think when I was flying to and from LA. I'm not sure if..."

"Yes?" Emma probed delicately. She wanted to know exactly how Meg felt about Max.

"Maybe it's just that marrying Frasier seems like the right thing to do. I've never been as romantic as you, but sometimes I wonder if...well, if I shouldn't have been swept off my feet. I used to think that I'd know right away when I met the right man."

"Love at first sight? Trust me, that doesn't work. I fell in love with Max the second I saw him."

"Yes. I know it's silly, but I used to believe in it. But when it never happened, I stopped expecting it to. And then Frasier came along, and everything felt so right...."

"It is right. You're not making a mistake. Unless you don't love him?"

"I do love him. It's just not...not overwhelming. I know I'm being stupid."

"Meg, are you changing your mind about the wedding?"

"No. Oh, no. That would be wrong. After all the work you and Frasier have put into it. All the guests. Daddy."

"Meg, you're the one who has to be sure. It's till death do you part."

Meg examined her coffee cup. "Let's get some wine instead, shall we?" She rose and took a bottle from her wine rack. "A nice Australian red. When we published *The Complete Book of Wine Tasting* I developed a real fondness for the Australian wines."

Emma let her uncork the bottle and pour out two glasses before she resumed their topic. "Meg, are you having doubts?"

"A few," Meg said with a sigh. "But that's normal, isn't it? Bridal jitters. I'm sure Frasier is the right man for me."

"He is," Emma assured her. He was, she told herself firmly. Max would never forgive himself if he abandoned Meg. She couldn't let Meg abandon him. He would feel responsible and Emma didn't want that. She wanted Meg and Max to be happy.

"A toast to the man of my dreams," Meg said.

The two friends clinked glasses, but from the faraway look in Meg's eyes, Emma didn't think she was toasting her groom. Emma drank and vowed that come hell or high water or an avalanche of toasters, she was going to see Max and Meg married. Even if she had to drag Meg kicking and screaming down the aisle.

13

The best man

A FURIOUS POUNDING at the back of the church grew louder and louder. Emma turned to look and saw an unknown man knocking at the windows, motioning for Meg to leave the altar and run away with him. "Don't do it," she tried to say, but she couldn't open her mouth. She realized she was holding cover film against her mouth and tried to push it away with heavy hands when she discovered it was her pillow and the pounding was someone at the door. She'd slept on the couch, insisting Meg take her own bed. The knocking continued as Emma pushed off the warm blankets, grabbed her robe, tied it around her and made her groggy way to the door.

"Who's there?"

"Jay."

Emma opened the door. Jay looked a mess—his shirttails were sticking out of his pants, his hair stood on end and his eyes were puffy. He pushed past her. "Where's Meg?"

"Asleep, I think." Emma yawned. "Although I'm sure all this noise must have wakened her."

"It has. I'm glad you're here, Jay," said Meg, who was dressed in a short black skirt with a matching fitted jacket and a white, man-tailored blouse, its large cuffs protruding and held together by cuff links. Emma was rather stunned by her friend's cool professionalism and a degree of sophistication she had never quite expected from Meg.

"I've been awake for some time and have made coffee. Why don't you both sit down at the dining room table and I'll serve."

Jay grabbed his sister by the shoulders. "Meg, you have to talk to me. Gary Watson mentioned something about you being upset by some records and that…Meg, I get the feeling they involve me!"

"They do," she answered calmly. "Now if you will sit at the table and drink your coffee, I'll tell you all about it." She left the bemused pair.

Emma shrugged her shoulders. "We might as well do as she says." She squeezed Jay's arm.

Meg served them and then sat down herself, but she didn't touch her cup. "I've been up for hours and phoned Frasier. I've been so confused by everything that's been going on. You're right, Jay. The records in L.A. clearly point to you being involved in the extra print runs."

"Meg—"

She held up her hand, stopping him, while Emma wondered where her controlled friend had come from. Meg seemed so different from when she had left to go to L.A. Or even last night. It was as if she'd made a decision. Surely she wasn't thinking of canceling the wedding? Emma immediately quashed that thought. That was her own wishful thinking. Besides, it wouldn't solve her problems with Max. If Meg left him, Max would be devastated. No, these two were getting married. Emma would make sure of it.

"At first, I couldn't believe what I had. And then I was so upset I wasn't thinking clearly. I'm sorry to say, Jay, that there was a moment when I doubted you. But Frasier showed me the truth. That you have to believe in the people who are important to you, even when the facts seem to point the other way."

"Frasier?"

"Yes, Frasier. He's a good man, Jay. You're going to have

o learn to accept that. He'd never do anything to hurt you or
me. I'm sorry for my momentary lapse, but weakness is, unfortunately, part of human nature. It's our better nature that makes us rise above it."

Emma felt every word strike her like a knife, cutting out all of her unreasonable, stupid dreams.

"Frasier has an idea. He should be here soon." As soon as the words exited Meg's mouth, there was another knock at the door. "Would you get that?" she asked Emma.

Emma walked across the living room to the door and opened it to Max. For a moment he looked at her in her robe and sleep-tousled hair, but his face remained impassive.

"Jay's here," was all she said as she moved aside to let him in.

"Good. That will speed up everything." He saw the brother and sister sitting at the dining table and made his way over to them. Bending down, he lightly brushed his lips over Meg's. Then he sat down and unzipped his portfolio. "I was up most of the night going through all the records again. Jay's name was in a lot of places it shouldn't be."

Jay started to say something, but stopped. Meg reached over and held his hand. Max continued, "Every time I checked one of the incriminating records, the same person had signed off on the film just before Jay."

"Who?" Emma asked.

"Jill Ellis."

"Jill!" Meg exclaimed. "She can't be involved. Why, she and Daddy...well, they're so happy together."

"The guilty person is someone at Scorpion Books, Meg. I'm sorry, but that's the truth. I admit it seems odd, but the motive could be purely financial. Do you know why she left her last publishing job?"

"Jill was freelancing for a couple of years, and before that the company she worked for went bankrupt. But that's not unusual," Meg hurriedly added. "Publishing is always pre-

carious and a couple of bad years can ruin a company. Why,
if we never hired anyone who worked for a company that
went belly-up, we'd only have half a staff."

Jay let go of his sister's hand and stood. He began to pace
off some of his nervous energy. "Still, it's possible she had a
hand in the unfortunate demise of the last company. If she
was involved, this could be history repeating itself. I know I
haven't cared much for Scorpion Books over the years, but I
do care now."

"But it's possible to care too much," Meg stated. "I've been
doing some thinking and have realized that I've poured too
much of myself into the business. No matter what happens
over the next few days, I'm going to pull back. Maybe take
some time off."

"Meg—" Max began.

Meg smiled at her fiancé. "If we're to be married, Frasier, I
think I should make you a higher priority than my work.
Don't you think so?"

"Yes," he said, but for a quick moment he looked at
Emma.

"Jay, you deserve a chance to show Daddy and everyone
at Scorpion what you're capable of without me being around
as a comparison. You should have your chance."

"But I don't want to run the company." Jay brushed his
hair out of his eyes impatiently. "You're good at being the
editorial director and the heir apparent, Meg. You love it.
The best part of Scorpion Books for me was meeting Sarah."
He flushed. "I think I've finally convinced her to give me a
chance. You have to believe me when I tell you I don't want
your job, Meg."

"Jay, I don't want to stand in your way."

"You're not. You never did. I may have blamed you in the
past, but that was only because I didn't know what I
wanted." He took a deep breath and stood taller. "I finally
know what I want to do with my life. Being at Scorpion, be-

ing around books and writers finally showed me my purpose. I'm going to be writer."

"My baby brother is going to be an author." Meg smiled at him and then hugged him.

"Yes." Jay looked at Emma and Max. "That night you caught me sneaking out of Sarah's office was me stealing back the manuscript I'd left on her desk earlier in the day. I wanted her to read it and give me her professional opinion. I also wanted to prove to her that I did have a purpose. That I could finish a project when it meant something to me. Before Sarah, and my realization that I wanted to write, I was never willing to commit. To give everything to something and someone I loved."

He looked away from them. "But that night, after I'd left my book in her office, I got scared. I was afraid Sarah would hate it, that she'd think I had no talent, so I went back and retrieved it. That's when you saw me. I was too embarrassed to tell you the truth."

Jay's mouth twisted in a half smile. "But I did give Sarah the book and she read it and thinks it has promise. It needs revisions, but Sarah says she has faith in me. And—" he beamed at them "—she is finally starting to trust us. I love her more than anything."

"Jay, that's so romantic. I wish I had someone who..." Meg stopped and looked around, as if she was really seeing them for the first time. "I'm happy for you, little brother. It seems we have several happy couples. Except for Daddy, if Jill is involved."

"Jill..." Jay shook his head. "I can hardly believe it. But why would she have forged my signatures on the documents?"

"To point the blame away from herself." Max stood. "It's only seven-thirty. Jill is rarely in the office before ten. I suggest we pay a call on her and find out what she has to say before we mention anything to Peter."

"Won't that tip her hand?" Emma asked.

"I want to finish this investigation before the wedding. Let's hear what Ms. Ellis has to say."

Jay and Meg both insisted on going with Max, as did Emma. She changed quickly, fluffed her hair with her fingers, put on some lipstick and raced out to join the trio waiting for the taxi.

All three remained silent, wrapped in thoughts and secrets—at least Emma was involved in her own guilty secrets—until the cab stopped in front of Jill's building. Jill lived in a co-op on the Upper East Side, a very exclusive neighborhood. "Wow," was all Emma could say as the doorman helped her out of the taxi.

"Tell Ms. Ellis that Meg Cooper is here to see her."

The doorman called up and then directed them to take the elevator to the eleventh floor. The old elevator with its handsomely scrolled wrought-iron door creaked its way to eleven. They turned right in the hallway, where Jill was waiting at her apartment door.

Catching sight of them, she frowned. "Is something wrong? Is it Peter?"

Meg assessed the woman coolly. Jill was wearing a bright pink silk robe that she recognized came from a very exclusive store. "Nothing is wrong with my father, but yes, something is wrong. Can we come in?"

Jill nodded and Emma entered the oval foyer with the rest of them. Several open doorways led off in different directions and a spiral staircase led to a second level. The entire apartment was painted in dark, rich colors, highlighting the woodwork and cornices. Jill led them from the foyer, passing a library-workroom into a sun-filled living room.

"This place is wonderful," Emma exclaimed.

"It's big for one person but I like a lot of space. Please sit down. Can I get anyone coffee?"

"No," Max said, and looked around.

Jill seemed to become aware that all of them were assessing her apartment, and she stiffened. "Then maybe you could tell me why you're here."

"Jill," a male voice shouted from the foyer. "I couldn't get the blend of Viennese Colombian you wanted, so I got the house special." A handsome man walked into the room and stopped in surprise. "We have company."

"Yes, these are my colleagues from work—Frasier Thorne, Meg and Jay Cooper and Emma Delaney, the wedding consultant. This is Jack Anders."

He smiled, his blue eyes crinkling, laugh lines etching his mouth as if this was a frequent occurrence. "Jill doesn't like to admit it, but I'm her ex-husband."

"Obviously you're still very close," Meg said suspiciously.

"We managed to remain good friends," Jill said coolly, "if that is any of your business."

"Shall I make coffee?" Jack asked.

"No," Jill answered. "My colleagues were about to explain what they're doing here."

Max took charge. "Peter Cooper hired me to investigate the recent thefts at Scorpion Books."

"Yes?" Jill didn't tap her foot impatiently, but her body language was just as hostile.

"I've also done a background check on you. This is a very expensive apartment, you take several vacations each year, yet your only clear source of income is your editorial position at Scorpion Books. And you don't have any rich relatives."

"So you naturally assume that I am guilty of embezzlement?"

"Oh, no, Jill," Meg insisted. "But we do have to question everything. And your name has unfortunately appeared on some documents that seemed at first to incriminate Jay."

"What?" Now Jill looked very puzzled. "My name? That can't be. I haven't had anything to do with the troubles at

Scorpion Books. I love my job. I care for your father. wouldn't want to hurt him."

"Then what is your ex-husband doing hanging around?" Meg demanded. "I don't think Daddy would be happy to know how comfortable he is here—waltzing into your apartment early in the morning with your favorite coffee."

Jill sighed. "I see I'm going to have to explain myself." She moved around the room, picking up a figurine from a sofa table. "You're right, I do like nice things. But I also like working at a job that I enjoy. I've always been good at books. Picking winners. Helping an author discover the story he or she wants to tell. Besides, I would have made a terrible lawyer or accountant. Those options just don't interest me."

She replaced the figurine. "Just before Jack and I decided to separate for good, we made one last effort to save our marriage by working together."

"I'm a playwright," Jack added.

Jill touched his shoulder briefly. "Yes, he is. And a talented one, but he hasn't had much luck so far. I think I fell in love with Jack because he's so creative. Not only can he write, but he's a talented artist. And I can write and I'm good at marketing, so we formed a small greeting card company. Sort of a cottage industry operating out of our homes."

"Jack and Jill," Emma interjected, realizing that she knew their business. When the group looked at her in puzzlement she continued. "Jack and Jill greeting cards. The cards play with fairy tales and legends and are very funny. I've bought them many times."

"Exactly," Jill said. "We decided to use the obvious connection to our names—which we'd hated all the time we were together as a couple—and the cards were popular almost from the start. Jack works here a couple days a week designing new cards and then I add my input and coordinate sales. We really are a two-person operation."

"Your greeting cards have brought you all this?" Max asked.

"Yes." Jill smiled in satisfaction. "The business has become extremely lucrative, but neither Jack nor I want to spend all of our time on cards. Jack continues to write his plays and I edit books. It all works out very nicely."

"But why did you never tell us?" Meg asked. "I'm so impressed by what you've managed to accomplish."

"I've learned that discretion is better. A lot of publishing companies, no matter how nice they seem, want you to devote yourself twenty-four hours a day to them. They feel like a betrayed lover when they learn that you have an outside interest and income. Soon everyone is looking at you in a different way. Wondering if you should be privy to all the information. Wondering when you're going to quit your job. I have no intention of leaving Scorpion Books, so I haven't told anyone."

"Not even my father?"

Jill sighed. "No, not yet. I will. If things become...more serious. Now you see where all my unexpected riches are from. Does that clear your suspicions?"

"Not entirely. I'm sorry," Max continued.

Jill grew angry. "Then go ahead and search my apartment and see if you find anything incriminating. I refuse to stay under suspicion like this."

"Jill, the man is only doing his job," her ex-husband said soothingly. "Go take a look around, you won't find anything. I've known Jill for a long time. She may like nice things, but that's it."

Max stood up. "I will take a quick look around, if you will excuse me."

Strained silence stretched until Emma couldn't take it. "M—Frasier will figure this out, don't worry."

Jill surveyed her coolly and then resumed her pacing. Emma opened up her briefcase and pulled out the guest list and special dietary requirements. She might as well try to get a little work done. With only three days to the wedding, and day one being the wedding, she needed to hand over the final numbers count and menu.

Meg pulled a manuscript out of her bag, but she only riffled through the pages, pretending to read. Jay picked up a magazine, while Jill continued to pace. All of them could hear Max walking from room to room, opening drawers and cupboards.

Surely he wouldn't find anything. Jill couldn't have betrayed Peter Cooper, the man who clearly loved her. Jill seemed to love him, too, but Emma no longer knew what to believe. She truly would be happy when she could leave what was turning out to be her own personal wedding from hell—forget the first one where Max hadn't shown—and begin her life anew.

A life without her silly fantasies about Max.

He would be a safely married man and she would find someone for herself. Someone practical and calm. Someone who understood her, but didn't send her into these ridiculous highs and lows of emotion. What she needed was stability. Just like Max and Meg were settling for.

Settling for?

Was Max settling for his love for Meg?

No, Emma was deluding herself again. But she suddenly felt hope as well.

With her, Max was out of control. In full possession of his feelings and passions. Maybe she should fight for her man.

Caught up in her thoughts, Emma lost track of how much time had passed until Max returned to the room, his face grim.

He held out his hands. "Cover film."

14

The mother-in-law?

"IMPOSSIBLE," Jill said. She grabbed the mechanicals out of Max's hands and studied them, her face growing pale. "Oh my God. It's the cover film for Zoe Dixon's book. This can't be." She looked so shocked that either she was a superb actress, Emma decided, or she was genuine. But she'd have to be a good actress if she was involved.

"I didn't do this," Jill cried. "I couldn't have, wouldn't have. Oh, what can I say, you have the evidence against me."

Jack walked over to her and put his arm around her shoulders. She leaned against him gratefully, while everyone else looked to Max. "Now what do we do?" Meg asked in a quiet voice.

"None of this makes sense." Max ran his hand through his hair.

"What do you mean?" Emma asked. If Max thought there was more to it, that Jill wasn't necessarily guilty, then what? Then who? First it had looked like Jay, now Jill. A glimmer of truth came to her. "Everyone who seems guilty has a very close connection to Mr. Cooper."

"Exactly." Max spun toward her excitedly. "You have it. All the clues that we've found have been laid out for us in plain sight. I found this in Jill's briefcase."

"Like someone wanted us to find them."

"Yes. First Jay, Peter Cooper's son. Then Jill Ellis, the woman he's involved with."

Jill pulled herself out of Jack's arms and turned to Max. "You mean you don't think I'm guilty?"

"As long as your financial story about the greeting cards works out, I don't see what motive you would have for stealing from Scorpion Books, from Peter Cooper. Do you love him?"

Jill blushed and looked down at her feet for a second before raising her chin. "Yes," she said firmly. "I love him very much."

"Motive is what has been missing here. I know that investigators usually look for opportunity, but in this case almost everyone has the opportunity. The only thing that seems to make sense is that someone wants to hurt Peter Cooper. I think we'd better go talk to him and figure out who."

"WHAT DO YOU MEAN someone wants to hurt me?" Peter Cooper demanded to the group assembled in his office. Emma had been afraid that Jack Anders would come along as well, but Jill had managed to talk him out of it.

"First all the clues pointed to Jay. Now they lead to Jill."

"Neither Jay or Jill would do anything to hurt me."

"I know," Max continued. "But someone does."

"I can't think who it would be."

"Does no one obvious come to mind? A business deal that went bad?"

"I've only ever invested in Scorpion Books, nothing else."

"A friendship gone sour? An unhappy author? An unhappy end to a love affair?"

Peter shook his head. "No ended friendships. There are always a few authors who are disgruntled, but I can't imagine one of them angry enough to pull off an elaborate scheme like this. The most they're usually capable of is a letter to the editor. As to bad love affairs, well, I haven't really been involved with anyone until I met Jill."

Emma realized the biggest change in his life recently had

been his falling in love. She felt like that fact was important, but couldn't figure out how.

"Well, then, what do we do?" Peter Cooper demanded.

"We set a trap," Max answered.

"DO YOU REALLY THINK this will work?" Emma asked once again.

"It has to." Max looked tired as he rubbed his jaw. He glanced at her quickly. "By the way, after this is over, we're going to talk."

"Max." Emma couldn't resist reaching out and touching his face, letting her fingers linger on his cheek. His hand shot out and grabbed her fingers, holding her to him. "There's nothing to talk about," she whispered. "You're going to marry Meg. You made a promise to her. You're a man who keeps his promises."

"But maybe my promise is wrong."

"No," she said firmly. "The last thing I ever wanted to do was to hurt either you or Meg. I'll admit that right after our almost-wedding I wanted to hurt you, but that's the past. I've pined for you for too long. It was good to finally meet again and for me to see that you'd begun a new life. To be perfectly honest, I think I was waiting for you to reappear in my life. A part of me believed we could have a happy ending, that you still loved me and everything would work out."

"I do love you."

Emma couldn't look at him. "No, that's your guilty conscience speaking. You think you've betrayed Meg, therefore you have to be in love with me. But it was only old feelings. Emotions that belong in the past. I'm not going to say I want us to be friends, but I do want you and Meg to be happy."

"Emma—"

"You two, together again," Mrs. Daley said scornfully from the door.

Max looked up at her and smiled with satisfaction. "I thought you might be working late tonight, Mrs. Daley."

"I came in to pick up some papers Mr. Cooper asked for."

"He's still here?" Emma asked. "I thought he and Jill were going out for dinner."

"I wouldn't know what Mr. Cooper's social plans are." Mrs. Daley patted her immaculately coiffed, dark hair and glared at Emma. "He wanted the second quarter's net sales figures from the chains."

Max took a folder from the pile of papers on his desk, which began a slow slid toward the floor. Both Emma and Mrs. Daley grabbed for the avalanche of files, managing to save most. "Heavens," Emma said, "almost a disaster."

"You should file your papers more often, then this wouldn't happen," Mrs. Daley said with a snort, and after depositing the pile back on the desk, she grabbed the folder she wanted. "Does Miss Cooper know you spend so much time together?"

"Of course I do." Meg joined them and kissed her fiancé on the cheek. "After all, they've been busy planning my wedding."

Mrs. Daley frowned at all three of them, turned on her heel and flounced out of the room.

"She saw it, didn't she?" Emma demanded.

"Yes, she did," Max concurred.

"I pulled the same number on Art Spiegle yesterday and Brenda Lau this afternoon, just like you asked me to." Art Spiegle and Brenda Lau seemed innocent after their reasons for their peculiar behavior had been revealed, but this time Max and his helpers weren't taking any chances. The bait was being offered to everyone.

Jay now seemed completely innocent. He had explained that the large cash deposits from across the country into his bank account were paybacks. On his twenty-first birthday he'd received a lump sum of two hundred and fifty thousand dollars. For once he'd been responsible and decided to help his less fortunate friends—offering loans to the new graduates to establish small businesses or buy a home. His investments were now paying off big time.

All day yesterday and today, Max, Meg, Peter, Jay and Jill had let several key suspects know that the cover film for their expected big blockbuster was hiding in their respective offices. After all, because of Peter's unusual security measures, the criminal couldn't always know where the film was. If Max was correct, the villain wouldn't be able to resist one last big strike, and what better way to hurt Scorpion than with what was almost guaranteed to be its next bestseller? A book expected to appear on the *Times* list in its first week of publication. Kathleen Drake's two most recent novels had debuted on the list and this book was the conclusion to her trilogy. Scorpion would be shipping so many copies, no one could get any kind of a handle on unexpected returns until it was too late. The thief or thieves could return hundreds of thousands of covers for *Wicked Surrender* and ruin what was left of Scorpion Books.

Thus the trap was laid out for their top suspects. The additional plan was for each of the collaborators to hide in his or her office tonight, waiting for the thief to make his move. Emma had offered to help as well, but there was little she could do.

She, Meg and Max retired to a nearby diner and were joined by Peter, Jill and Jay. Emma tried unsuccessfully to enliven the dispirited meal, but they soon broke up, each planning a different and hopefully unobtrusive entrance back into Scorpion and a carefully chosen hiding place.

"Do you really think this will work?" she asked Max.

"I hope so. Hiding in closets isn't my usual style, but I want this issue settled before..."

"Before your wedding."

"Yes. I can't really go on with my life until this is cleared."

"At least Mr. Cooper knows it's not Jay or Jill."

"Does he?"

"What do you mean?"

"What if we don't capture anyone tonight? I've seen how worried Peter looks. The guilt will then naturally shift back to his son or his girlfriend."

"Oh." Emma absorbed that news. "Is there nothing I can do?"

Max sighed and stopped in front of Meg's apartment building. She was walking a few feet behind them, arm in arm with her brother. Meg was going to change into something more comfortable before heading back out. "I think you've done enough."

Emma felt cold and sad, but she nodded and waited for Meg to join her in the elevator. Emma had overheard a few words of the siblings' conversation; Jay had been asking Meg for advice about how to woo Sarah. Jay was also feeling guilty that they were keeping Sarah out of the loop in regards to what was happening at Scorpion Books. While Max had claimed that he had no reason to suspect Sarah, he'd also insisted he wanted to keep knowledge of the trap limited to as few people as possible. Knowing Max, Emma realized that he had probably also dropped the bait to Sarah, just in case, but he wasn't about to tell Jay.

Once Meg had left for her adventure, as she sadly called it, Emma couldn't settle down. Questions of what she wanted kept invading her thoughts no matter how much she tried to push them away.

Finally she realized she wasn't going to be able to sit in Meg's apartment wondering what was going on at Scorpion Books. She changed into leggings and a long black sweater and headed back out. At the Scorpion building she faltered briefly, but then continued on in. She had no intention of getting in anyone's way, or of becoming a suspect herself, but she had to be there for closure. To discover who the guilty party was. To watch the last obstacle to the marriage of Meg Cooper and Frasier Thorne be removed.

From the times she'd spent talking to Amy at the reception desk, Emma knew there was quite a big space under the desk. Amy had told the story of how the previous receptionist had been discovered sleeping off a hangover under the desk one morning as the phones rang and rang.

By lying flat on the floor and placing her eye against a seam of the wooden desk, Emma could get a clear view of a small corner of the lobby. She would be able to see anyone walking in or out.

After an hour in the cramped quarters, her bum was sore and cold from resting on the hard marble and she was developing a major knot in her back. She was almost relieved when she finally heard footsteps. Pressing her eye against the seam, she saw Art Spiegle enter the building with a man she didn't recognize. At least she didn't think she'd ever seen him before—she couldn't be one hundred percent certain about the men who'd been talking to Art when she'd spied on him before.

They walked to the elevator and were gone, while Emma wished she'd brought a cell phone with her to warn Meg. If Art was after the cover film, then he'd be heading to Meg's office, since she was the one who had set the trap for him. Suddenly Emma was scared. What if Art tried to hurt Meg? Max had insisted that with this much money involved, anyone could be dangerous. Emma rubbed her arms, trying to get warm as she worried about Meg. Surely somebody would hear what was happening? She doubted it. Max and Jay were on different floors.

Emma crawled out from under the desk and ran to the elevator bank and watched the indicator stop on 7. Meg's floor. Emma had no choice; she took the second waiting elevator and pressed six. She'd run up the last flight in case Art Spiegle and his companion heard the elevator.

Out of breath, she opened the fire door to the twelfth floor as quietly as possible and peered up and down the hallway. With no one in sight, she tiptoed down the corridor toward Meg's office. Halfway there she heard footsteps and ducked into the corner holding the photocopier.

She wondered when she had developed this propensity for hiding, and then realized that she'd been hiding her true feelings for the last eight years.

Art and his companion stopped by the coffee machine and he poured a cup of the dregs for the other man. Their hushed conversation was too faint for Emma to overhear no matter how she strained. Then she heard footsteps.

"Who's there?" Meg asked.

Art started guiltily and stuffed a large manila envelope, more than big enough to hold cover film, into the recycling bin as Meg walked into the small coffee area.

"I didn't realize you were back from L.A." Art said.

"Yes. Zoe Dixon should be able to finish the book without me now and I really did need to return for my wedding. It's less than three days away."

"Yes, er, congratulations. This is Bernard Hoffmann, one of our illustrators. He painted the inside step-back image on Kathleen Drake's last romance."

"That was a beautiful picture," Meg enthused. "You're here working awfully late."

"Been out of the office a lot in the last few days, had some paperwork to catch up on." Art rubbed his neck and looked around guiltily.

Emma realized she could slip out of the photocopier area and around the wall to where Art and Meg were conversing. She did. She wanted to know what was in the brown envelope that Art was trying to ignore, but wouldn't leave without either. She gave them a few minutes to exhaust all their small talk, then walked in to find Meg fixing herself a cup of coffee very, very slowly.

"You're here, too?" Artie snapped irritably.

"Wedding plans," Emma answered airily. "Is there any coffee left for me?"

"You can have mine," Meg offered, practically thrusting the cup into Emma's hands.

"I couldn't!" she replied, adroitly sidestepping. "You need it. But I'll make myself a fresh pot." She emptied the old coffee grounds, put in a new filter, tore open a new bag of coffee and cleaned out the pot. Art, Meg and Bernard watched her in silence.

Bernard looked at his watch. "Shouldn't we be going?"

"Er, yes, er, I think I forgot some papers in my office. I definitely forgot my papers." Art half bowed. "If you ladies will excuse me." His hand shot for the brown envelope as he straightened and turned, but Emma was faster. She slammed the heel of her hand over the envelope, pinning it in place.

"What's this?" She picked up the envelope as Art began to turn red.

"Nothing." He reached for the envelope, but Emma held it tightly against her. "That's mine. Give it back." He took a menacing step toward her, looming over her.

"I left some documents here," Emma answered sweetly, "I think this is mine."

"No. Give it back now. Or..."

"Or what?"

"It's important," he said beseechingly, darting his eyes toward Meg.

Meg was staring at the envelope. "We have to look, Art. I'm sorry. With everything that's been going on, with someone stealing from us, I have to see what you're hiding in the envelope."

"No, Meg, please. You've known me a long time. I'm telling you there's nothing incriminating there. I'm not the person you're looking for. Please don't look inside the envelope."

Meg shook her head. "I'm sorry, Art. I have to. Give it to me, Emma. I'm the one who should look."

Art buried his face in his hands as Meg opened the envelope and pulled out the mechanical for a cover. At first she seemed shocked, but as she studied the picture more closely, her lip trembled and her eyes began to shine. "Oh, Art, how sweet!" To Emma she said, "It's a romance cover, except they've superimposed my face and Max's onto the couple. She's even in a wedding gown."

"You've ruined the surprise," Art grumbled.

Meg kissed him on the cheek. "This is so sweet. I won't breath a word of it to Max. He'll be touched."

They let Art and Bernard leave—he was the artist who had done the work on the wedding cover—and Meg asked, "What are you doing here?"

Emma was abashed. Once again she'd messed up. "I couldn't just wait to find out what was happening, so I hid in the lobby. When I saw Art and his mysterious and menacing friend—do all artists look like gangsters?—heading to your floor I got nervous and followed them."

"That was really thoughtful, Emma," Meg declared. "I guess I'd better head back to my stakeout." She rubbed a knot in her shoulder. "This is going to be a long night. Adventures aren't nearly as much fun as I thought they would be."

Emma agreed with those sentiments exactly as she returned to the lobby. When she looked down at her hiding spot, she realized she just didn't have the energy to crawl back under the desk. Instead she plopped down on the receptionist's chair and glumly contemplated her future.

She really was making a mess of everything. Only two more days and then she was out of here. Meg and Max would be married. No more silly romanticizing, either. Emma was going to become completely practical about her life. And she was going to think some more about the franchise deal she'd been offered—maybe her insistence on the personal touch so she could indulge in each and every wedding was a poor business decision.

She was so lost in her thoughts, slumped so far down in her chair, that she realized the stealthy figure heading through the lobby hadn't noticed her presence. That was strange; Meg could have sworn she hadn't heard the elevator. As she looked at the person's retreating back, she noticed the trendy backpack. Now that, too, was unusual. It didn't match the conservative attire.

She bolted upright as she realized what she was seeing.

Emma called after the thief, who stopped and then very, very slowly turned to face her.

15

Another bride's groom

"IT'S YOU." Emma rose from her chair and walked around the desk to confront the culprit. She didn't fully understand, but was beginning to put all the facts together. "You're the one who's been trying to ruin Scorpion Books, to hurt Peter Cooper."

"Yes," Mrs. Daley agreed as she moved toward Emma. "After all my years of service, devotion and love, he's betrayed me. He deserves to feel my pain." Fury crossed the woman's face, making her look fierce and dangerous, and Emma took a step backward into the console. A few moments ago, when she'd first realized that the faithful secretary was the woman behind the thefts, she'd felt only surprise and resignation at the sad truth, but the insane anger on Mrs. Daley's face frightened her. Emma realized how alone she was. Only Meg knew she was in the building, and since she was holding her own private stakeout, Meg wouldn't miss Emma until sometime tomorrow.

Don't be ridiculous, Emma thought, calming herself. She was letting her overactive imagination take control. Deliberately, she relaxed her shoulders and raised her chin. "Hurting the man you love won't bring him back to you."

Mrs. Daley's eyes flashed. "This is my life. I'm the one who decides whether or not I want revenge, not some little bridal consultant who dreams of weddings and romance and happy endings, yet is in love with a man who is marrying someone else. Don't try to look innocent with me. I've seen the way you look at Miss Cooper's fiancé and the way he looks at you when he thinks no one sees. I see. I *know*." Mrs. Daley poked her finger at Emma. "I know what it's like to have some scheming hussy set her sights on my man."

"Peter Cooper loves Jill Ellis."

"No, he doesn't. She's bedazzled him, tricked him! She made him leave me. If it wasn't for Jill Ellis everything would be like it always was. You're just like her. Stealing another woman's man. How could you?" The last sentence came out as a threat.

Emma became more and more nervous during the woman's tirade. This was no longer the efficient and pleasant woman who had been so easy to overlook. How often had Emma more or less ignored her, as did almost everyone else? They had all ignored the obvious pain she was suffering.

Emma wiped her sweaty palms against her thighs and began to make a small sideways move toward the door. If she could get outside, she'd run. She didn't really believe Mrs. Daley would hurt her, but the crazy look in the woman's eye told her it was better to be safe than sorry.

"You're right," Emma said softly, wanting to keep Mrs. Daley calm. "I do love Mr. Thorne. But he loves Meg, and they're getting married. I wouldn't do anything to hurt them." She edged toward the door.

"Don't lie to me. I've seen you catting around him, tempting him."

"No. What I never told anyone is that we had a past. We were involved once, a long time ago."

"You knew him before?" Mrs. Daley asked suspiciously.

"Yes. Eight years ago. We were in love."

"Your lies won't get you out of this."

"I'm not lying," Emma insisted desperately as the other

woman kept following her every move. "We almost got married."

That stopped Mrs. Daley as she considered Emma distastefully. "He was the groom who stood you up at the altar?"

"Yes," Emma said gratefully, for once glad of her infamous story and the gossip from it that always surrounded her. "But that's done now. Whatever you may have sensed between us was old feelings." She was almost at the door, and kept up her soothing patter. "I used to love Mr. Thorne. But in two days Meg and Max Thorne will be married. I'll be gone. Just like I'll be gone right now." She grabbed the door handle and pulled it open to freedom. She saw Mrs. Daley open her mouth, but she didn't wait to hear what the woman had to say.

Emma ran, straight into a wide and solid chest. Thick arms clamped over her and held her immobile.

"Emma, I'd like you to meet my son Arnold," Mrs. Daley announced proudly. "Arnie, be careful with the little girl, I haven't decided what we're going to do with her yet."

The man grunted and maneuvered Emma into the lobby. Emma screamed into the man's flannel shirt, but all she got was a mouthful of cotton. She spit it out and was momentarily disoriented when Arnold picked her up and turned her around.

"Arnie, be careful," his mother scolded.

"Now what?" Emma asked unsteadily.

"I need to think. Stop annoying me."

Arnie twisted her arm roughly and Emma pressed her lips together to halt her yelp of pain.

"Let me go. Nothing bad has happened yet." She looked pleadingly at Mrs. Daley. Surely the woman wasn't really going to hurt her? At the mad look in her eyes, Emma shivered.

"That's true, my dear, but nobody knew it was us. When

you've been at one company for as long as I have, it's criminally easy to find weakness."

"It's only money."

"So far," Mrs. Daley agreed pleasantly, rummaging through her purse. She pulled out a gun and pointed it at Emma. "But now you know the truth and I don't want to go to jail. Plus I have to protect Arnie. He was only helping me, like any good son would help his mother. He's always been a good boy. I can't let you hurt him." She raised the gun a little. "Peter may have betrayed me—" her voice cracked "—but Arnie never will."

Emma tried to make her brain function, but all she could do was focus on the gun. It looked so big in Mrs. Daley's hands. Big and powerful.

"I won't say anything. I won't tell anyone about you," she managed to say in a choked voice.

"Yes, you will." Mrs. Daley shook the gun at her in disagreement. Emma grew cross-eyed watching it. "The Coopers are your friends. And then there's Mr. Thorne. No, you'll have to come with us. If you say anything or make any funny moves, Arnie will break your arm." Mrs. Daley picked up her knapsack, so incongruous with her elegant image. She smiled at her son and Emma. "Okay, ready to go?"

Emma moved her feet automatically, a little surprised that her body was still able to follow her jumbled brain's directions. What was going to happen? What if she never saw Max again?

With Arnie practically dragging her, and Mrs. Daley following close behind, the three of them exited the building onto Broadway. The passersby gave no notice to Emma, so tightly sandwiched between mother and son as they led her toward a Ford Escort illegally parked next to a fire hydrant.

Mrs. Daley opened the passenger door of the two-door, maroon car. "Get in the back seat."

Emma did as she was told, realizing there was no way she

could escape from it. Nor could she try to knock out Arnie
and take over the wheel with Mrs. Daley in full control of the
gun. "Are you going to kill me?" she had to ask. That question had been going round and round her brain ever since
sweet, little Mrs. Daley had pulled out the weapon.

"Not as long as you don't make it necessary. Arnie isn't
going to jail, so if you behave and let us sell this last cover
we'll put our escape plans into action and you'll be free. It
will be too late for anyone to stop us. Or find us. But if you
interfere, if you decide to play hero, then I'll do whatever is
necessary. And you know that I'm a woman of my word. I'm
not afraid."

"No, you're not," Emma agreed, sitting back, relieved that
her life wasn't in immediate danger. She chose to believe
Mrs. Daley's words. Now that she thought about it, the clues
pointing to Mrs. Daley's involvement with the thefts were
obvious. She had access and a damn fine motive: a woman
scorned. Emma could relate.

As the car weaved through the traffic, Emma felt incredibly tired. All the events of the past two weeks settled upon
her and it seemed like too much to have to keep herself together any longer. First the emergency wedding, meeting
Max again, the thefts, her unresolved feelings for Max... Suddenly a truly horrible thought hit her and jerked her upright.
"The wedding," she spluttered. "I can't miss the wedding!"

"The wedding is the least of your problems at the moment," Mrs. Daley said from the front seat, refusing to turn
around.

Emma wrapped her arms more tightly around her and
leaned back into the seat. "Then you've never been around a
disgruntled bride." A gun-wielding lunatic or an angry
bride. Emma debated which was worse.

The bride.

MAX FROWNED OVER the sales figures and rubbed his fore-
head. He could feel a headache building. If only his trap last

night had worked. All he'd gotten was no sleep and a migraine. He'd been convinced the thief wouldn't be able to resist taking the bait.

Max was getting married tomorrow.

The headache began to pound and he opened a drawer, looking for aspirin. He found the bottle and was destroying the childproof cap when Meg walked in. "Oh good, you got your bottle open. I need three." She held out her hand and Max poured the tablets into her palm. Before he could pour her a glass of water, she gulped them down dry. He took his own medication and then they stared at each other.

"Well."

"So."

He used to be able to talk to Meg so easily. In fact, he still needed to tell her everything. But if he did, he'd hurt her. And he didn't want to do that. He'd vowed to himself that he'd never hurt Meg. He'd already hurt enough people in his life.

"Have you seen Emma today?" Meg asked.

"What? I thought she was with you."

"No, after she left here last night, I thought she went back to my apartment, but she didn't. I even asked my doorman this afternoon if he'd seen her."

His heart began to race. "What do you mean, she was here last night?"

"You know Emma. She couldn't let us handle the stakeout and not be a part of it. She hid in the lobby."

"How do you know this?"

"When she saw Art Spiegle head up to my floor, she ran ahead to warn me. But it was nothing."

Max tried to keep the panic out of his voice. "No one has seen Emma since then?"

"Not that I know of. I thought she was working on the final wedding details...or that maybe she was with you...."

"What do you mean by that, Meg?" His throat closed as he tried to get air into his lungs.

Meg looked at a spot on the wall behind him. "Oh, nothing, really. It's just that you two spent so much time together..."

"On the wedding."

"Yes. The wedding. Frasier, you are sure about tomorrow, aren't you?" Meg chewed her bottom lip nervously.

"Yes," he said, wondering why he couldn't tell her the truth. *Coward.* But first he needed to find Emma. "The receptionist," he said. "Amy always talks to Emma several times a day. I think I saw them making napkin rings or something together one day."

He pressed zero on the phone, connecting him to Emma's biggest fan. But Amy revealed that she hadn't spoken to Emma all day and that Emma had had a lot of calls, none of which seemed to have been returned. "That's not like her, Mr. Frasier. She usually phones in for messages. I thought maybe something was wrong. With the wedding."

Max took her off speakerphone before she could say anything more that Meg might overhear. Just what did he think Amy might say?

"She hasn't called in," he said to Meg when he hung up.

"Frasier, I'm worried. That's not like Emma. Do you think...could something have happened to her?"

He was very afraid that Emma's propensity for investigating, for not leaving things damn well alone might have gotten her into trouble.

"Frasier, I have to ask...you and Emma didn't have a fight or anything, did you?"

He looked at Meg, wondering what she knew or suspected about him and Emma. "No, we didn't have a fight. Let me call Beth at your father's house and find out if she's heard anything."

He picked up the receiver again, but his office door opened to reveal Beth and the aunts.

"Have you seen Emma?" Beth asked. "She was supposed to meet us half an hour ago but she never showed."

"Oh, Beth, we were hoping she was at the house with you," Meg cried.

"What's wrong?" Primrose demanded, her Southern voice sharp as steel. "Emma wouldn't disappear without a good reason."

"Last night was the last time anyone saw her," Meg said. "She was here at the office."

"We set a trap for the thief last night," Max clarified.

"And Emma was here as well? Well, clearly she found the thief, but then the thief caught her." Primrose shook her head. "Not a very good trap."

"How dreadful. We have to rescue her," Daisy said to her sister.

"Of course," Primrose replied. "I'm sure Mr. Thorne will be able to help us. Who are we going after?"

"We don't know."

"But surely you must have suspects. Emma assured us you were a very good investigator."

"Apparently not good enough." Damn, what was he missing? Who was missing? Max looked around at the crowd gathering in his office, drawn by their excited voices. Jill Ellis and Jay Cooper had already joined them. Peter Cooper walked in. "What's going on?" he demanded.

"It's Emma—we can't find her." Meg looked like she might cry. "Daddy, this is terrible. What if something has happened to her? I used to think the worst thing would be if we lost Scorpion Books, but now I know I was wrong."

"Nothing will happen to Emma. Frasier will make sure of it."

Max had the wild urge to ask everyone to call him by his

real name, but he realized that panic was setting in. *Think.* He needed to focus on— "Where is Mrs. Daley?"

"She went home early because she wasn't feeling very well. Plus she wanted to finish her preparations for the wedding tomorrow."

Dread filled him. This must have been what Emma felt like eight years ago when he stood her up. She would have been worried about him. How could he have hurt her like this? He'd been stupid eight years ago, but if things turned out right now, he'd make it up to her.

What about Meg?

He'd worry about that a little bit later. Right now he needed to think, to figure out this damn case. "Last night, did anything go missing?"

Peter Cooper answered, "No, all of the cover film is here. Mrs. Daley checked the jackets for me and locked them away."

"Pull them out. I want to see them."

"Of course." Peter stood and left the room.

Max turned to the others. "Did any of you see anyone else in the building last night?"

"Just Art Spiegle and one of his artists, like I told you."

"I think Mrs. Daley was working late last night," Jill offered. "I'm not sure, but I thought I saw her leave."

"Mrs. Daley?" Max demanded. He was very afraid that was the answer. He didn't wait to hear any more, but ran out of his office to follow Peter Cooper to the locked storeroom, one floor down. Movement was the only thing that helped his agitated nerves.

The publisher had just unlocked the door and was checking the shelf where the book cover mechanicals were kept in their folders. "Check all the film," Max ordered.

Peter looked at him curiously, but remained silent and started looking through the brown envelopes. Jay arrived to help. After a couple of minutes, Jay raised his head. "There's nothing in this folder." He held up the brown envelope marked *Wicked Surrender* by Kathleen Drake.

"It's Mrs. Daley—she's the one who's behind all this. She's always had access. Why didn't I see that before?" Max took off again, determined to catch the woman before she made her escape, before she could hurt Emma.

"I'm coming with you," Peter Cooper shouted after him, and caught up with Max at the elevator.

"This could be dangerous."

"It's my company. And somehow, if Mrs. Daley is involved, I think it centers around me. I need to be there. I would never forgive myself if Emma was hurt."

Max didn't argue and they didn't speak again until they were in his car and racing through the streets. Peter gave him the address of Mrs. Daley's apartment in Queens.

"I can't believe it's her," was the only thing Peter said during the drive.

Max didn't say anything.

On a pretty, tree-lined street Max pulled up in front of number 327. Peter pointed out Mrs. Daley's front apartment. "Her place is on the second floor. How do we handle this?"

"We go upstairs and find out." He rarely carried a weapon with him; it was hardly ever needed in his line of work. Max wondered exactly what they were walking into. Surely he was wrong. Mrs. Daley was just a sweet woman who worked for Scorpion Books.

"She has a son," Peter added. "I've seen him once or twice, a big man. Maybe he needed money."

"Maybe." They walked up the steps to the second floor. In a cheery, white-painted hallway, Max stood on the welcome mat and pounded on the door.

"Who is it?" Mrs. Daley asked.

Max motioned for Peter to answer.

"It's Peter Cooper."

The door opened; Mrs. Daley was all-smiles. "How sweet

of you to come and see how I'm feeling! Really, my headache was never that bad that you needed to come all this way...." She saw Max and frowned. "Oh, it's you. What are you doing here?"

"My job." He entered the apartment.

Mrs. Daley ignored him and turned her attention back to Peter. "It's such a long ride over. Can I get you a drink or something?"

"Yes, tea would be nice," Max answered as he scanned the room.

"I was speaking to Mr. Cooper."

"Tea would be wonderful," Peter agreed.

"Please sit down. I won't be but a minute."

Peter followed Mrs. Daley into the kitchen and Max heard their voices, Mrs. Daley's as excited as a schoolgirl's. He took the opportunity to walk through the apartment, but there was no Emma. What had he expected—that he'd find her doing a kidnap note in calligraphy?

But he couldn't get rid of the feeling that she'd been in this apartment and that Mrs. Daley was the person he'd been hunting for. He looked around the comfortable place again. Like many apartments in Queens, Mrs. Daley's living space took up the entire floor of a large building, an apartment meant for growing families. Her decor was homey—old, solid furniture covered with crocheted afghans. The oak pieces gleamed with polish. On the mantel above the fireplace, he found photos of Mrs. Daley as a young bride with a large, slightly intimidated-looking groom, then a series of baby pictures and school pictures of a young boy. Her son, Arnold. What was Max missing?

He opened the doors to the two bedrooms, checking the closets and under the beds, but no Emma. She wasn't in the apartment.

Peter came out of the kitchen carrying a tea tray including

cups and a plate of cookies. He shrugged at Max and mouthed, "Nothing."

Mrs. Daley followed. "Please sit down. I've always believed a good cup of tea can do wonders for the constitution. I'm so looking forward to the wedding tomorrow. Meg will make such a beautiful bride."

"We're all glad that Frasier will be joining our family. I couldn't have asked for a better son-in-law."

"Hmm." Mrs. Daley made a peculiar noise and sipped her tea. Max felt her eyes boring into him. When he looked up she smiled coldly at him. "Loyalty," she said sternly to him. "Being true to your wife is the most important gift you can give her. No running after other women."

"Of course not," he said, but felt his face flush.

"Don't try to fool me. I've seen the way you look at that hussy Emma."

"Hussy?" Peter Cooper interjected. "My dear Mrs. Daley, you are mistaken. Emma is a wonderful girl."

"You're just as blind as all men." Mrs. Daley spoke passionately to Peter. "You can't see a temptress when she's putting out all of her lures. Why, Jill Ellis is just the same."

"You're jealous of Jill Ellis. That's it!" Max smacked his hand on the coffee table and the teacups jumped.

"Be careful, young man."

Max turned to Peter. "I finally understand Mrs. Daley's motives. But if she doesn't have Emma here, where could she be?"

Peter looked puzzled. "Why is Mrs. Daley jealous?"

"She's in love with you."

"That can't be."

"It is," Mrs. Daley said proudly. "I'm not ashamed of my feelings. That Jill Ellis isn't nearly good enough for you."

Peter sat back in his chair. "I don't—"

"Mrs. Daley, where is Emma?" Max interrupted to ask.

The woman sipped her tea and refused to answer.

"I think Arnold has an apartment in this building as well."
Peter shook his head in bewilderment. "This is all so strange,
but I think Arnold lives on the third floor. In the back."

"I told you that the last time you drove me home. I never
keep any secrets from you, Mr. Cooper." The woman's
mouth straightened into a hard line. "Leave my son out of
this. He's always been a good boy."

"Where is he?" Max could barely keep the panic out of his
voice.

Peter took Mrs. Daley's hand. "Please tell him what he
wants to know."

She seemed to crumple in front of their eyes. "Apartment
3C."

"Stay here with her. Make sure she doesn't call him," Max
added. Peter looked slightly stunned as Max ran out of the
apartment and up the steps.

Three C was in the back of the building. He tried the knob,
but the door was locked. Acting out of fear, he kicked in the
lock and rolled into the apartment, stopping behind the sofa.

"What?" A large, meaty man stumbled out of a kitchen
chair. Max saw the small, cheap linoleum table next to the
back window and Emma tied to the other chair. Fury over-
took him as he launched himself on Arnold. The two of them
fell on the ground together.

Arnold was big and strong, but Max had surprise and anger on his side. Arnold tried to push him off, but Max managed to wrap his fingers around the man's thick neck and
squeeze. His actions seemed to happen in slow motion. Arnold hit him on the shoulders and then on his head, but nothing mattered to Max except that this man had threatened
Emma. He squeezed harder.

Eventually Arnold's punches grew weaker, but Max's
rage didn't allow him to loosen his grip. Then he felt something kick him on the back, and a body fell between them.

He let go. Emma had landed with a loud thump on the

floor and he pulled her into his arms. "Emma, my God. Are you all right? What happened?" Dazed, he looked around the room.

"Max," she gasped. "I had to make you stop. I was afraid you were going to kill him."

He could have, he realized. He'd been completely out of control. Gently he helped Emma upright and saw that her hands and legs were still tied. She smiled ruefully at his expression. "I hopped over here like a kangaroo." He looked down at the unconscious Arnold. "I had to do something."

Silently he untied her and then he pulled her into his arms and held her tightly against him. She felt so right. It was like coming home. "Emma, I was so worried about you. When you disappeared, when no one knew what had happened to you, it was like a part of me had died. I was so scared." He held her face between his hands, as if he couldn't believe she was really in his arms. In her eyes, he saw a vulnerability and a sadness he'd never seen before.

Suddenly he knew. "Oh my God. That's how you felt when I..."

"When you left me. I never knew what happened to you. I was hurt and scared and worried. Your telegram helped a little, but since it was so unlike you, sometimes I didn't even believe you'd sent it. Sometimes I thought maybe you'd been killed."

"That telegram *was* unlike me. I thought it might make you hate me. That if you hated me, you'd be okay."

Emma smiled tremulously, her feelings for him spread across her expressive face. "I could never hate you, Maxwell Thorne."

Unable to resist, he wrapped her even tighter in his arms. He couldn't say the words to her, but he couldn't stop holding her, either. "I'm going to kiss you," he said, giving her a chance to break away.

"Every hero who rescues the damsel in distress should

kiss her," Emma said with a smile, and leaned her head closer to him, so that their lips were only a breath apart.

"I'm no hero."

"I disagree," Emma said. "You'll always be my hero. Now just kiss me, please."

Max kissed Emma. Nothing could have stopped him from kissing her. He'd been so worried about her, and he felt even more guilty finally understanding how Emma had felt eight years ago. Now that he had her in his arms, now that his lips were devouring hers, he never wanted to let her go.

With his mouth and his body, he told her all that. He kissed her passionately, desperately, wanting to remember her taste, the feel of her in his arms. Emma was soft and strong, vulnerable and determined. She was everything he'd ever wanted.

Finally Emma broke off the embrace and stepped out of his arms. He let her go, feeling bereft. She looked at him, pain in her eyes. "Thank you for rescuing me." They were silent for a minute, as Max realized Emma was waiting for him to say...something. But he couldn't. No matter how he felt about her. He wasn't going to break his promise to Meg.

Emma looked away. "What about Mrs. Daley?" she asked.

"Peter Cooper is downstairs with her."

She smiled sadly, took his hand and squeezed it gently. "Then we'd better go join them and wrap up this nastiness."

He let her lead him away from Arnold, away from his lack of control. It was ironic that Emma had stopped him from totally losing control, since he'd always believed she was the greatest danger to his self-control. Now that he knew the truth, was it too late for them?

Back downstairs, Peter and Mrs. Daley were seated awkwardly on the sofa. Mrs. Daley held herself regally upright. "You found her. Did you hurt Arnold? Where is he?"

"He'll be fine." Frasier stopped in front of Peter. "Do you want me to call the police?"

"Call the police. It's over now," Mrs. Daley said wearily. "Just leave me alone."

"You've been part of the company for almost twenty years! I want an explanation," Peter stated.

"An explanation!" She came back to life. "Twenty years I took care of you. Who made sure you ate properly and took care of yourself after your wife died? I did. Who arranged all of your social engagements, told you what the mood of the employees was like? Who advised you about personnel and promotions?"

"You did. I've always appreciated everything you've done for Scorpion Books."

"I've never done anything for Scorpion Books," Mrs. Daley declared. "I did it all for you. For you." She slumped on the couch.

"Me?"

"I loved you. I took care of you. And then what did you do? You fell for that—that woman."

"You did this because you love me? You can't love me."

"She does," Emma interjected. "I've spent the last day with her and have heard all about you. I've even seen the scrapbook she keeps on you. Mrs. Daley loves you."

Peter looked puzzled, then he grew concerned. He moved to take her hand but stopped. "I'm sorry. I never realized."

"I know. I never really expected you to love me back, but you always said..."

"That I loved you. That I wouldn't know what to do without you. Surely you knew that it was only an expression. I never meant...damn, I'm only making this worse."

"*I love you. I wouldn't know what to do without you.* I knew you never really meant them, but I liked to hear the words. It was enough. I thought you would always mourn your wife and that I would be the woman in your life. Until Jill came along."

"I love Jill," Peter said sadly. "I am sorry."

"I know. And I've had all day to think about everything...and well, I'm glad you caught me. I don't really want Scorpion to fail. We didn't even sell the Kathleen Drake cover. You'll find it on the desk. Phone the police, but please leave Arnie out of this. He was only doing good for his mother. He doesn't deserve to be punished."

Peter shrugged and continued sitting. "I'm sorry."

"Do you want me to call the police?" Max asked. He still had his arm around Emma; he just couldn't let her go.

"No. No police."

"What?" Mrs. Daley turned to him in surprise.

Peter took her hand. "I can't send you to jail. You are part of my family. And I do love you, just not the way you want."

Mrs. Daley burst into tears and Peter pulled her against his chest. "You're so good," she sobbed. "And I hurt you so much." She stood suddenly and went to the closet, pulling out a suitcase. "Here, here's almost all the money. Take it back. I never knew what to do with it. Take it. It's yours."

Peter examined the briefcase. "This helps. Frasier, can you think of some way we can get this back into the company without too many questions from the IRS?"

"I'm sure I can work up some ideas."

"Good. Then we'll do that. We can also make up a story for the staff. I'll need to tell only a few people the truth." He turned back to Mrs. Daley. "That way you can decide what to do."

She nodded slowly and Emma realized that while Jacqueline Daley had gained her freedom and what some would consider a too-light sentence, she was losing what she had valued most in life. She would no longer be spending every day with the man she loved.

A fate that Emma, too, seemed to share.

Get me to the chapel…

THE MORNING OF THE Cooper—Thorne wedding was picture perfect. Emma sighed as she studied the clear blue sky. Birds sang, flowers bloomed, the band tuned and waiters clinked glasses and china.

It was going to be one of the most beautiful weddings she'd ever organized. She should be proud of herself. Instead, she was afraid she was going to faint. Emma weaved through the tables, refolding a napkin, moving a centerpiece, until she was at the bar. "Pass me one of the champagne bottles," she asked the waiter. "The bride needs a drink to settle her nerves."

He winked conspiratorially at her, uncorked the bottle and handed it to her with two glasses.

Primrose and Daisy waved to her from the gift table. Emma waved back, but didn't stop to talk. Everyone had talked more than enough yesterday—about Mrs. Daley, about the thefts.

After Max's behavior toward her, his obvious concern, Emma had kept her distance from him. In his over-emotional state he might have said or done something irrational. Something he would regret later.

What she'd reminded herself over and over again was that she was doing the right thing.

Maxwell Thorne—no, *Frasier* Thorne and Megan Cooper

were getting married in less than two hours. And Emma was going to toast the happy couple.

She walked back inside the house, into the library.

All of the details were organized. She could sit here and get quietly sloshed if she wanted.

Pouring a glass of bubbly, she toasted the happy couple. Then she toasted herself. She was about to break down in tears when she decided she was stronger than that. This day was going to be as bad as her aborted wedding, but she had lived through that. And made a success of her life. She'd do the same now. This time she'd know that Max was married, that there was no point in dreaming about him. In believing that one day he would realize they were meant for each other.

She toasted the end of her romantic dreams.

Maybe she needed to find herself a new career.

No, she was good at this one. She loved weddings. She loved happy endings. And she truly believed that she'd have one of her own someday. She put her glass back down on the desk and stood. She was no coward. Moreover, she had a job to do. In the distance she heard the band practicing the first dance. The tempo was off; she needed to go speak to the band leader. She was going to carry off this wedding and smile her way through it. No matter how much it hurt.

"MEG, WE NEED TO TALK." Max knocked quietly on Meg's bedroom door.

There was a rustle of skirts and the door opened a crack. "Frasier? What are you doing here? It's bad luck for the groom to see the bride before the wedding." Belying her words, she opened the door and let him inside. "But I've never much believed in superstitions."

At the sight of his bride, Max stopped. Meg was a picture of sophisticated elegance and beauty in a V-necked, cream gown, tightly fitted bodice and simple flared skirt. His throat tightened. "You look beautiful."

"Thank you. Good enough to marry?" she asked with an odd note in her voice. Meg walked back to her dressing table and sat down on the chair, fingering a scrap of ivory-colored paper.

"That's what I need to talk to you about."

"I rather thought you did. I've been waiting for you."

"You know," Max said suddenly.

Meg sighed. "I've suspected for several days. Ever since I got back from L.A. Yesterday I looked through the old mementos I kept in the attic. I keep everything, did you know that?" Max shook his head. "No, I didn't think you did. There's a lot of things we don't know about each other, aren't there?"

Meg frowned at the piece of paper she was holding and then at him. "Don't you think we should know more about each other? I asked you if you'd ever been married. I never asked if you'd *almost* been married." She handed him the paper, which he now saw was a wedding invitation. An invitation to the marriage of Emma Grace Delaney and Maxwell Frasier Thorne. "I was invited eight years ago, but I was in Europe." Meg looked at him expectantly.

"I'm still in love with her." It hurt to say the words to Meg, but she deserved the truth. She deserved a man better than him as a groom. Meg deserved a man who was overwhelmingly in love with her.

"Yes. I can see that. What do you want to do?"

"Meg, I really thought I loved you. That I would be a good and faithful husband to you. But then Emma came back into my life and I've just realized that what we have...it's not enough."

"So you're willing to stand me up at the altar and go after Emma? What makes you think she'll take you back?"

"I don't know if she will. But I intend to spend the rest of my life trying."

Meg's shoulders slumped as she looked at herself in the vanity mirror. "First, Mrs. Daley steals from Scorpion Books because she loves my father. Now my fiancé is abandoning me because he's in love with my friend. I'm not sure if love is worth the cost."

"Yes. Yes it is." That was the one thing in this whole crazy situation that he knew was true.

"And what we had was nothing even close to that. Well then, I'm not going to give you my blessing exactly, but I do agree we shouldn't get married." She stood up and motioned toward the back of her gown. "Would you mind undoing these buttons? I won't be able to reach them."

He began working the buttons, hardly able to believe what was happening. He clasped his hands on her shoulders. "Meg, I'm sorry."

Meg lowered her head. "I know."

He turned her around to face him. "I wish there was something better I could say."

She raised her chin, her face calm. "I think you'd better plan out what you're going to say to Emma. And to our guests."

"What do you mean?"

"I mean that I'm leaving you to take care of this mess. To explain to my father. I have a suitcase packed. As soon as I've changed out of my wedding dress—" her voice broke, then she took a deep breath "—I'm out of here."

"Where are you going?"

"To have an adventure."

He looked at her with dawning realization. "You were never going through with the wedding."

"No. I've been waiting for you all morning. I was sure you'd come to your senses and stop this."

"And if I hadn't?"

"I suppose I would have done something—I hadn't decided what. Shown you the old wedding invitation and demanded an explanation? Not shown up? I had several delicious scenarios in mind."

"Yes, I guess you did." He leaned down and kissed her on the mouth. "Goodbye, Meg. Take care of yourself."

"Goodbye, Frasier. Max." Meg wiped at the corner of her eye and Max decided he should leave quickly. "Wait, I almost forgot. I got something for you...and Emma. Just in case."

Max took the object and smiled when he saw what it was. It was funny how he could be happy and sad at the same time. Sad that the dreams he and Meg shared wouldn't be coming true. He hoped she would find someone who loved her as desperately as he loved Emma. He leaned down and kissed her cheek. "Have a good adventure."

"NICE WEDDING." His breath rustled warm against her back and Emma willed herself not to react.

"I think I've done a nice job." She turned to face him and then had to restrain herself from reacting to how handsome and wonderful he looked in his tuxedo.

"A wedding you would have liked to have yourself?" He was looking at her with a curious expression on his face.

"I had my wedding," she said coldly, growing angry at him. She was finished with Maxwell Frasier Thorne.

"I wish we could do it again."

"We can't! It's too late. You're marrying Meg."

Emma still couldn't read his expression, but she wanted him to leave her alone. He was breaking her heart all over again.

He touched her cheek, but she moved her head away. His shoulders slumped slightly, but Max looked at her with determination. She felt her heart begin to pound, as he began to speak. "I was wrong eight years ago. I should have given you a choice. Believed that you would have loved me enough to forgive me. To wait."

"I would have waited." She couldn't help but tell him the truth. She would have waited forever. She had waited for him. Today was the day she stopped waiting.

"I realize that now. I'm not sure I believed it then. I thought you loved the successful Maxwell Thorne. I wasn't sure that you'd love me no matter what."

Emma stepped way from him, furious at him for his stupidity. "You said you never contacted me because you didn't want to ruin my life!"

Max sighed. "That's what I convinced myself. But I'm not sure that was the real reason." He stepped closer to her. "But if you loved me now, I'd believe."

"I can't love you. You're marrying Meg."

Max took a deep breath. "I love you. I don't love her."

Emma grabbed his arm as if to drag him down the aisle. "You're marrying her."

He caught her hands between his. "I love you."

"Stop saying that. Don't you know how long I've waited, wished, longed for you to say that to me? How can you say it now? How can you be so cruel?" She was afraid she was going to cry, so she looked at their hands, joined together.

"Emma, listen to me. There's no reason I can't say it to you now. I love you. I'm willing to stand up in front of all these people and tell them exactly that." He pulled her hands against his heart. "Tell me you love me too. That you still want me."

Emma couldn't believe what he was saying. Had she had more of the champagne than she'd thought and was now suffering a delusion? When she shook her head, Max let go of her hand and took a step toward the assembled guests who were beginning to assume the seats. Emma grabbed him and pulled him back. "Don't you dare. Don't you dare hurt Meg! You can't embarrass her like this."

He turned back to her, his face alight with emotion. "If it's really love, then I'd be willing to do anything for you. Including embarrassing myself in front of all of these guests. Or waiting eight years for you to agree to marry me. Marry me!"

"Max, stop this." She tried to pull her hand away from his. "You're only making everything worse."

Max shook his head. "Yesterday, when I didn't know what had happened to you, when I was afraid something terrible might have happened, I realized how you must have felt when I left you. I told you that, remember?"

Emma nodded, feeling both jubilant and sick to her stomach. Whatever Max was feeling had to be temporary—because of yesterday. She couldn't stand in the way of Max and Meg's happiness. She never wanted to put another woman through what she'd been through herself. "Now you know. That's good enough. Leave me and marry Meg."

"I'm not marrying Meg." He took possession of her hand once again.

"You can't stand her up! I won't let you do something like that to her."

Max's mouth twisted in a rueful grimace. "I already have."

"No." Emma pulled her hand free and slapped him hard across the face. He reeled back slightly and rubbed his red cheek.

"Oh my God," she said. "I'm out of control. You always did this to me, Maxwell Frasier Thorne."

"No." He stepped toward her. Emma backed up, but she hit a tent wall and Max pulled her into his embrace, wrapping his arms around her like a vise. "You always made me lose control. That's what I was so afraid of. I love you."

She felt a small part of her melt. She wanted to believe his words, but she couldn't.

"Yesterday, when I thought I might lose you, I realized

that was the worst thing that could ever happen. That's when I knew marrying Meg would be a mistake. I love you." He lowered his head and kissed her, softly and gently as if he treasured her. Emma kicked him in the shins and he let go of her.

"Ouch, that hurt, damn it!"

Now he was back to the Max that she preferred, the arrogant, controlling man. "You are a pigheaded fool," she said. "How dare you propose to me on the day you're supposed to be marrying another woman?"

He took another step toward her and she backed up once more. Unfortunately, she hit the tent wall again. "I'm making up for lost time," he said.

"What about Meg?"

"She's gone. Don't look at me like that. I didn't do anything to her. She's been having doubts all along and her time away from me in L.A. confirmed her feelings. And I think she suspected something about us."

Emma hung her head, unwilling to meet Max's gaze. "Oh, no. It was my fault."

Max lifted her chin, his dark eyes serious. "No, Emma. It was no one's fault. If Meg and I had gotten married it would have been a mistake. A mistake that we would have both tried to work on, but we would have been unhappy—and too proud to admit it." He smiled ruefully. "Meg has gone in search of adventure."

"Meg always wanted to have an adventure...." Emma said softly.

"Emma." Max stopped, a frown crossing his face. "I love you. With you I have no control. I don't know what is going to happen next or what I'm going to do next, but I do know that I want to spend the rest of my life with you. Before, you said you still loved me...do you?"

Emma gazed at this man she had always loved. He looked

unsure of himself, but determined, and she felt a sudden lightening of her spirit. "Yes. Yes, dammit, I still love you."

Max kissed her quickly. "Good, that's what I needed to hear. We can take as much time as you want before we get married. I'll prove that you can trust me."

"Max, I know that I can trust you. You might do a lot of stupid things, but they'll always be because you believe you're doing the right thing. So—" she took a deep breath "—I'll marry you as soon as we can get a license and a minister. And a dress."

He smiled wickedly. "How about right now?"

"We can't."

"We can." He pulled out Meg's wedding gift to them. "Meg gave this to us."

Emma read the paper and realized it was a marriage license for Emma Grace Delaney and Maxwell Frasier Thorne. "Meg gave you this?" she asked in confusion.

"Yes. Darling, she wants us to be happy."

Emma buried her face against his chest, and Max patted her on the back. "Darling, sweetheart, don't cry."

That made Emma want to cry even harder. "I never thought you'd call me those words again. I need your handkerchief."

Max handed it over and she wiped her eyes and blew her nose.

"Are you okay now?"

"Yes." Her smile trembled a little but she was starting to feel better and better. A bubble of joy seemed to be building inside her and she thought if it grew any bigger she might just float away.

"Then let's do this properly," Max said as he went down on one knee and clasped her hand between his.

"Max, this is silly." She tried to tug her hand away.

"No, it's not. It's romantic. Be quiet and stop struggling while I do this. Will you, Emma Grace Delaney, do me the great honor of making my life complete by becoming my wife?"

"Oh," Emma said as she checked to make sure her feet were still on the ground. It had to be Max holding her that kept her grounded. Which is what she wanted for always, she realized as she looked him.

"Well?" he prodded, looking a trifle nervous. "If you say yes we could have the wedding right now and begin our life together."

"I need a dress," she insisted. "I am not getting married in a blue bridesmaid's dress. I have my professional reputation to consider."

"There has to be a dress among all the stuff you carted here from Philadelphia. Emma, please...?"

"Well, yes, I think I might have the perfect dress." She waited, wanting him to agonize just a little longer.

"Emma, won't you please say yes?"

"Yes," she said. "Definitely yes." He stood and pulled her into his arms and kissed her until they were both breathless. "Yes, Max, I will marry you—but only because I'm not going to let you ruin another wedding I've organized. I can't be the bridal consultant who failed to get Maxwell Frasier Thorne to the altar twice! Imagine what people would say."

She smiled at him with all the love in her heart shining on her face. "Obviously, to save my reputation as the best bridal consultant ever, I'll just have to marry you!"

Epilogue

They lived happily ever after...

"I THINK THAT WAS the most beautiful wedding I've ever seen," Daisy Winslow confided to her sister.

Primrose dabbed at her eyes. "It was certainly unexpected. Imagine Meg abandoning her groom at the altar and the bridal consultant stepping in to marry him. These Northern girls have a very peculiar sense of decorum."

Daisy eyed her sister critically. "You know better than that, Primrose. Clearly Miss Delaney and Maxwell Thorne—oh my, but I keep thinking of him as Frasier—had a very *significant* past. You were telling me only a couple of days ago that you thought something *funny* was going on."

"I meant Meg. When a bride doesn't show for her own wedding you have to wonder."

"Well, I did wonder about Emma and Mr. Thorne. They were spending so much time alone together... And you could see how ecstatic the pair of them were up at the altar exchanging their vows. Emma truly was a beautiful, glowing bride."

The sisters sighed in unison.

"The groom looked like he couldn't believe his good luck," Primrose agreed.

Daisy scanned the crowd eagerly, waving at Sarah and Jay. "This certainly has to be the most unusual wedding we've ever been to! When Peter Cooper came out to make the announcement that there had been a slight change of plans, why, I thought that he and Jill Ellis might be joining the couple on the walk down the aisle. How do you feel about that idea, sister?"

Primrose smiled. "You know me too well. At first I was horrified, but our dear sister has been gone a long time and, no matter what Daddy used to say about Peter, he is a good man and he does deserve to be happy. I hope they make their announcement soon. It would give us another excuse to come to New York."

"Be careful, you might begin to like this Yankee pace of life," Daisy teased.

"Don't be ridiculous." Primrose sniffed. "But I am interested in how we invested our money. We need to visit every once in a while to check on how Scorpion Books is doing."

"Otherwise we'd be bad businesswomen," Daisy agreed enthusiastically. "Why, we didn't build our present-day fortune from that tiny little amount father left us."

"Exactly. If you leave men to their own devices, who knows what fool ideas they'll get up to? I was never so shocked as to learn that Daddy had gambled all our money away."

"But we did all right." Daisy patted her small evening bag proudly, as if it contained their very sizable fortune.

"Yes, we did. Thank goodness for the stock market!"

"And Bill Gates," Daisy said with a giggle.

The sisters smiled as Jay and Sarah walked over to them. Jay handed each of his aunts a glass of champagne. "Let's toast to the unexpectedly happy couple," he said, and raised a glass of ginger ale. When Primrose raised a brow, he shrugged lightly and linked his hand with Sarah's. "This beautiful woman has agreed to think about my proposal if I can prove I can behave."

"Oh Sarah, you would be the best thing that ever happened to Jay if you said yes," Daisy exclaimed, and kissed the younger woman on the cheek. "For our sake, please do consider joining the family."

"I'm thinking about it, especially since, for some reason I can't figure out, I am madly in love with Jay. After today's wedding, I've begun to think that maybe real love can win out after all." She shook her head. "I rather suspected there was something between Emma and Frasier—I mean Max—but I would never have imagined..."

"None of us did," Peter Cooper agreed as he joined the group, accompanied by Jill. "Not every father would be happy to be hosting a wedding at which his own daughter didn't show, but now that I've stopped worrying about Scorpion Books..." He paused meaningfully. Everyone in this group had been told the truth; everyone else had been told that Mrs. Daley was taking early retirement. "Well, I began to think about my daughter," he continued. "Meg wasn't nearly as much in love with Max as she should be. I was too much of a coward to ask her about it. Luckily, she made up her own mind." Peter raised his own glass. "Here's to Meg's adventure."

Everyone toasted. "Look!" Primrose pointed to the stage. "Emma is getting ready to throw her bouquet."

Max walked with Emma to the center of the stage, and then, as if he couldn't resist, he pulled her into his arms and kissed her. He continued to kiss her as the crowd began to hoot and holler.

"Oh, my," Daisy said. "They're so much in love."

Sarah laughed out loud at the sight of the delirously happy newlyweds. "I think they're planning to make up for eight years in one night, so I suggest we single girls rush up the front to catch the bouquet before our happy bride and groom disappear on us." Sarah took Jill's elbow and called the two sisters to join her. In a flurry of movement, Jill, Sarah, Primrose and Daisy made it to the front of the stage where the happy groom was still kissing his bride.

"Throw the bouquet," Daisy shouted, and Emma finally broke free from her bridegroom's grasp. She blushed prettily as Max reluctantly let her go.

"Throw the bouquet so we can leave," he whispered into her ear, and then gently bit it.

"Stop that," Emma admonished very unconvincingly. "Max, there's a lot more to this wedding business than just saying 'I do.' We're supposed to circulate among the guests."

"Not at this wedding," he said firmly. "It took me too long to say 'I do.' Eight years too long. Now I want you all to myself and all alone."

"Oh," Emma breathed as her face lit up with love and desire. Max caught her against him and kissed her again.

"For heaven's sake, at this rate, she'll never throw the bouquet," Jill complained as the bride and groom continued to kiss passionately. Finally Emma broke away, turned her back to the crowd of women and threw—

"This way," Jill shouted.

"Over here, girlfriend," Sarah yelled.

Max scooped Emma up in his arms and swept her off the dias and straight into their new life together. It truly was the best wedding Emma Delaney Thorne, bridal consultant extraordinaire, had ever been to.

"Darn," Daisy complained as she felt an elbow knock her out of the way. "I missed it. These darn young kids."

"Got it," said Primrose, pulling her elbows back in. She held up the bouquet and grinned from ear to ear. "I've always wanted to catch one of these. I guess this means I'm next to walk down the aisle!" She sighed and looked dreamily at the flower arrangement as if imagining her own nuptials. "There's nothing I love more than a good wedding!"

Don't miss Meg's search for adventure in
THE ADVENTUROUS BRIDE available fall 1998

**It's hot...
and it's out of control!**

**It's a two-alarm Blaze—
from one of Temptation's newest authors!**

This spring, Temptation turns up the heat. Look
for these bold, provocative, *ultra*-sexy books!

#679 PRIVATE PLEASURES
Janelle Denison
April 1998

Mariah Stevens wanted a husband. Grey Nichols
wanted a lover. But Mariah was determined.
For better or worse, there would be no more private
pleasures for Grey without a public ceremony.

#682 PRIVATE FANTASIES
Janelle Denison
May 1998

For Jade Stevens, Kyle was the man of her dreams. He
seemed to know her every desire—in bed and out. Little
did she know that he'd come across her book of private
fantasies—or that he intended to make every one come true!

***BLAZE!* Red-hot reads from Temptation!**

Look us up on-line at: http://www.romance.net   HTEBL

Take 4 bestselling love stories FREE

Plus get a FREE surprise gift!

Special Limited-time Offer

Mail to Harlequin Reader Service®

3010 Walden Avenue
P.O. Box 1867
Buffalo, N.Y. 14240-1867

YES! Please send me 4 free Harlequin Temptation® novels and my free surprise gift. Then send me 4 brand-new novels every month, which I will receive before they appear in bookstores. Bill me at the low price of $3.12 each plus 25¢ delivery and applicable sales tax, if any.* That's the complete price and a savings of over 10% off the cover prices—quite a bargain! I understand that accepting the books and gift places me under no obligation ever to buy any books. I can always return a shipment and cancel at any time. Even if I never buy another book from Harlequin, the 4 free books and the surprise gift are mine to keep forever.

142 HEN CF2M

Name	(PLEASE PRINT)	

Address		Apt. No.

City	State	Zip

This offer is limited to one order per household and not valid to present Harlequin Temptation® subscribers. *Terms and prices are subject to change without notice. Sales tax applicable in N.Y.

UTEMP-696 ©1990 Harlequin Enterprises Limited

HARLEQUIN®

Temptation

*A small town
in Georgia. A family
with a past. A trilogy
packed with sensual secrets
and private scandals!*

Meet Savannah, Tara and
Emily—the McBride Women.
They've come home to put the
past to rest. Little do they
suspect what the future has
in store for them!

Don't miss these sultry, sexy,
Southern stories by bestselling
author Gina Wilkins:

#668 SEDUCING SAVANNAH
—January 1998

#676 TEMPTING TARA
—March 1998

#684 ENTICING EMILY
—May 1998

Southern
SCANDALS

Available wherever Harlequin
books are sold.

Look us up on-line at: http://www.romance.net

HTESS

HARLEQUIN® Temptation.

It's a dating wasteland out there! So what's a girl to do when there's not a marriage-minded man in sight? Go hunting, of course.

Manhunting

Enjoy the hilarious antics of five intrepid heroines, determined to lead Mr. Right to the altar— whether he wants to go or not!

#669   *Manhunting in Memphis*—
Heather MacAllister (February 1998)

#673   *Manhunting in Manhattan*—
Carolyn Andrews (March 1998)

#677   *Manhunting in Montana*—
Vicki Lewis Thompson (April 1998)

#681   *Manhunting in Miami*—
Alyssa Dean (May 1998)

#685   *Manhunting in Mississippi*—
Stephanie Bond (June 1998)

She's got a plan—to find herself a man!

Available wherever Harlequin books are sold.

Look us up on-line at: http://www.romance.net   HTEMH

KEY TO MY HEART

Unlock the secrets of romance just in time for the most romantic day of the year— Valentine's Day!

Key to My Heart
features three of your favorite authors,

Kasey Michaels,
Rebecca York
and Muriel Jensen,

to bring you wonderful tales of romance and Valentine's Day dreams come true.

As an added bonus you can receive Harlequin's special Valentine's Day necklace. FREE with the purchase of every *Key to My Heart* collection.

Available in January,
wherever Harlequin books are sold.

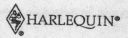

HARLEQUIN®

PHKEY349

THE MEN OF BACHELOR CREEK

Alaska. A place where men could be men—and women were scarce!

To Tanner, Joe and Hawk, Alaska was the final frontier. They'd gone to the ends of the earth to flee the one thing they all feared—MATRIMONY. Little did they know that three intrepid heroines would brave the wilds to "save" them from their lonely bachelor existences.

Enjoy

#662 CAUGHT UNDER THE MISTLETOE!
December 1997

#670 DODGING CUPID'S ARROW!
February 1998

#678 STRUCK BY SPRING FEVER!
April 1998

by Kate Hoffmann

Available wherever Harlequin books are sold.

Look us up on-line at: http://www.romance.net   HTEBC